Arianna Snow's
Novels

The Lochmoor Glen Series

"*Patience, My Dear* is an enthralling, well crafted, superbly written 'page-turner' of a read, fruitfully exposed to the impairing remembrance and encounter of a first young love when nearing mid-life many years later. *Patience, My Dear* is very strongly recommended for readers searching for a superbly authored telling of an intricate and entertaining tale involving a love consumed memory and an ever-deepening mystery."

"A comedy of errors held together with taut suspense and biting dialogue, *My Magic Square* is a delicious pleasure from beginning to end."

"Unwelcome visitors make their residence nearby, and there's a reason why they're unwelcome. *Threaded Needles* follows two amateur detectives whose bond of blood is unbreakable as they try to find out just what suspicious character Ian MacGill and his associate are planning. The resulting adventure is entertaining and enthralling. *Threaded Needles* is highly recommended for community library mystery collections."

"A compelling human drama unfolds, making *Blessed Petals* a very solidly recommended read."

"*Without a Sword* is another entry into the Lochmoor Glen series, and does the series justice."

"Another exciting thriller from Arianna Snow, *Kade* is not a read to be missed for fans of the series."

"A gripping read of drama, *Please, Tell Me* is a top pick and very highly recommended."

—Midwest Book Review

Geoffrey's Secret

A NOVEL

Arianna Snow

Golden Horse Ltd.
Cedar Rapids, Iowa

This book is primarily a book of fiction. Names, characters, places and incidents are either products of the author's imagination or actual historic places and events, which have been used fictitiously for historical reference, as noted.

An Original Publication of Golden Horse Ltd.
P.O. Box 1002
Cedar Rapids, IA 52406-1002 U.S.A.
www.ariannaghnovels.com
ISBN 10: 0-9772308-9-9
ISBN 13: 9780977230891

Library of Congress Control Number: 2011930899
First Printing
Volume 10 of *The Lochmoor Glen Series*

Printed and bound in the United States of America
by Publishers' Graphics, LLC

Cover: by Arianna Snow
        Photo by L. Vanourny
        Printed by White Oak Printing, Lancaster, PA

♥
In Memory
of

Baron

The loving companion of
Lorette, Todd, Jake
&
Kazimir
♥

My Special thanks to:
God

KAE
(editorial)

family and friends
(support)

Momma and Daddy, KAE
(bookkeeping and packaging)

HIRAM GEOFFREY MCDONNALLY
FAMILY TREE

PATERNAL GRANDPARENTS
CAPTAIN GEOFFREY EDWARD MCDONNALLY
CATHERINE NORTON MCDONNALLY

FATHER
CAPTAIN GEOFFREY LACHLAN MCDONNALLY

UNCLE
EDWARD CALEB MCDONNALLY

MATERNAL GRANDPARENTS
ALEXANDER THOMAS SELRACH
SARAH GLASGOW SELRACH

MOTHER
AMANDA SELRACH MCDONNALLY

SISTER
HANNAH RUTH MCDONNALLY

NIECE
SOPHIA RUTH SIERZIK

HUSBAND: RAHZVON M. SIERZIK

BROTHER: GAELON SIERZIK

CARETAKERS
ALBERT ZIGMANN
ELOISE ZIGMANN

SON - GUILLAUME ZIGMANN

FRIEND: TRINA DUNMORE

FRIENDS
DANIEL O'LEARDON

LIVIA NICHOLS

NAOMI BEATRICE (MACKENZIE) MCDONNALLY FAMILY TREE

PATERNAL GRANDPARENTS
JEREMIAH NORMAN MACKENZIE
OCTAVIA HILL MACKENZIE

FATHER
NATHAN ELIAS MACKENZIE
DAGMAR ARNOLDSON MACKENZIE (STEPMOTHER)

MATERNAL GRANDPARENTS
JAMES HENRY SMITHFIELD
IRENE CLEBOURNE SMITHFIELD

MOTHER
BEATRICE SMITHFIELD MACKENZIE (Birdie)

BROTHER
JEREMIAH JAMES MACKENZIE

DAUGHTER
ALLISON SARAH O'CONNOR

HUSBAND
EDWARD CALEB MCDONNALLY

HALF-BROTHER
HENRY STRICKLAND (SON OF CECIL AND BEATRICE)
    WIFE: PEARL   SONS: MARVIN, CONRAD

FRIENDS
HARRIET DUGAN
JOSEPH DUGAN
HENRY MCTAVISH (Tavy)

MARYANNE AND BRUCE WHEATON
    DAUGHTERS:
    WILMOTH, MARVEL, CORINNE, JEANIE, DARA, MARTHA

The Chapters

Chapter 1

"Handcuffs?"

"Come down, come down,
My pretty bird,
That sits upon the tree;
I have a cage of beaten gold,
I'll gie it unto thee"

—Anonymous

In his mid-thirties, Hiram McDonnally, wealthy pacifist, was doing as much as possible to assist the local farmers while their family members were engaged as soldiers fighting the Germans in Belgium. Exhausted from a long day of chores, he sat down at his desk in the McDonnally mansion to commence with his other obligations as a prominent businessman.

Livia Nichols, Hiram's soul mate and tentative fiancée, stopped by his study. "Hello, darling. How did it go, today?" she asked, walking to his desk.

"I sincerely hope that Eloise has not prepared chicken for dinner." He pulled a few files from the left top drawer.

"A problem with the chickens at the Ogilvie farm?" she asked cautiously.

Hiram sat the papers down, leaned back, and let out a sigh. "Livy, our involvement in the war is necessary. Knowing that there will be thousands of men and women giving their lives, under the most deplorable of conditions, my insignificant discomfort with the carnage at the Ogilvie farm on slaughter day, will be overcome within a day or so."

"I am sorry, love. Well, I shall let you get back to your work. Shall I ask Eloise to bring you some tea or something?"

He scooted his chair back to the desk. "I am very well, thank you. What do you have planned until dinner?"

"Uh...I have to speak with Rahzvon about the plans for my school's play-yard."

He offered an unfavorable glance. "Play-yard? I provided space in the west wing for your school; I said nothing about a play-yard."

"Hiram, you cannot expect the children to be

kept inside all day. They need fresh air."

"Very well, go, convert my home into a monstrous nursery," he grumbled, picking up an envelope and removing the contents.

Livia leaned over, kissed his forehead and left the study. She went directly to the kitchen where the aroma of boiling chicken soup met her at the entrance.

"Oh no, Eloise, that is not what you are serving tonight, are you?"

"It is not?"

"Hiram has experienced a dreadful day at the Ogilvie farm and would prefer something other than poultry for dinner."

"Slaughter day, eh?"

"Yes."

Eloise put down the spoon and stopped stirring. "I thought it would be good for the master; it has healing qualities...but I shall prepare an alternative."

"Thank you. Have you seen Rahzvon?"

"He was in the garden with Sophia."

"Thank you and sorry about the soup. You really are a dear."

Livia exited through the back door to the garden where Rahzvon was standing by the gate to the back acreage and waving to his pregnant wife, Hiram's niece. He turned to Livia when she arrived.

"Blasted, Livia, Phia is going to speak with Guillaume about a nursery in the east wing." Guillaume was an aspiring young architect who lived with his parents, the caretakers—Eloise and Albert Zigmann. "Livia, this has to stop. I appreciate the accommodations, but Phia and I need a home of our own."

"Have you checked out all the possibilities?"

"I took her to every location within an hour and a half from here. Nothing suits her."

"Given enough time, surely something will be available."

"After our *third* child," he muttered. "I want to sit at the head of *my* table, even if it hangs from the ceiling."

"I know. I am sure that it will all work out. Well, I have some free time. Can we talk now...about the letter that you mentioned?"

Rahzvon nodded. "Do you think Hiram would mind if we used his study?" He started towards the door.

"He is in there working, as we speak."

"Very well, then let's talk here. It is private enough. Please have a seat, Livia."

The two sat down on the concrete bench. She glanced nervously toward the house. "I do feel guilty for using the plans for the play-yard as an excuse to speak with you. I am not in the habit of lying to Hiram...stretching the truth a bit, perhaps, but that is all."

"You did not lie to him; here are the plans." He waved them before her.

"But we already discussed them at length, yesterday. I must say, although Hiram objects to sacrificing any more property to the school, I adore your little garden suggestion to teach the children how to farm."

Rahzvon laughed. "I think Hiram would differ with you on your use of the term 'farm'." His smile vanished. "Livia, about this letter—it is actually only a brief note. I think that you should know that my interest in it is partially responsible for the injury to my hands. The extra time that I took to retrieve it from the desk delayed Phia's and my escape from the fire. It was foolish and irresponsible on my part, but I felt that another person's life was being threatened, as well."

Livia looked confused as it was even of greater importance than she had imagined.

"Phia nearly discovered it in my pocket after our escape, but I had the opportunity to have Guillaume discreetly remove it and return it to me later."

"You entrusted *Guillaume* with it?"

"I had no choice." Rahzvon awkwardly removed the note in question from his pocket with his lightly bandaged hands and presented it to Livia.

She trembled slightly while she gently unfolded the paper.

To the reader of this:
Know this—my imprisonment here and my
possible demise is the sole responsibility
of Mr. McDonnally.   —Avera S.

"*Hiram?*" Livia gasped.

"Well—?"

"This is absurd! Where did you get this?" she demanded.

"As I said, beneath the table at the cott—"

Livia left the bench and glared at Rahzvon, "Surely, you do not believe that this is authentic?" she scoffed. "Why it is nothing less than preposterous!"

"Please, Livia, sit down."

"Sit down? I will not. I am going to show this to Hiram, at once!"

Rahzvon quickly grabbed her forearm. "No!

Livia, hold on and hear me out. Please. Please, sit down."

Livia did, albeit reluctantly and still scowling.

"I know that this is upsetting, but you haven't had time to think it over, as I have. It could be real—a sincere plea."

Livia's eyes widened with fury.

"Livia, before you think that I am making an irrational assumption, consider the possibility that Hiram may not be the McDonnally charged."

"Then whom?"

"There are only three candidates in this part of Scotland. It could be...Edward."

"Edward?" her voice rose. "Please excuse me, but are you as daft as the author of this drivel?"

Rahzvon rolled his eyes.

"Edward is no more capable of imprisoning someone, any more than you or I," she scoffed. Her jaw dropped. "Oh! Perhaps it is Hiram's father, Geoffrey," she whispered.

"He *was* in the military, but soldiers have moral ethics about taking prisoners. Besides, he has been dead for years."

Livia clamped her hand to her mouth, "What if she was his—?"

"Livia that would have been ages ago."

"Well, I *know* it was not Hiram." She stared at the ominous paper in her hand. "It cannot be. I know him. I love him. Yes, he loses his temper on occasion and behaves a bit irrationally at times."

"A *bit* irrationally?"

"He is a decent, kind man; he is assisting with all that farm work, day and night."

"Some of the most notorious criminals have lived double lives, offering charitable community service."

Livia bit her bottom lip. "There is nothing you can say to convince me that Hiram is capable of such cruelty."

"There were many years during which you had no contact with Hiram. It has been said that he was very disturbed and resorted to drinking on several occasions."

"No, no." She shook her head. "He could never imprison any—" She stopped and scowled at the note. "No, let us forget it," she pleaded and left the bench. "Let sleeping dogs lie, as they say."

"Yes, but how can we? How can we live in the same house, knowing this? I *do* realize the consequences for the clan if this is brought to light. It would affect all of them, not only the men—Phia, Hannah, and Naomi. I am not sure as to what to do. I dare not do anything that jeopardizes Phia's condition."

"And Hiram—he is already near exhaustion. If we must, we should wait until after your child is born, after the war," Livia offered.

"This woman may be alive and captive somewhere; her life hanging in the balance, Livia."

Rahzvon stood beside her. She began to quiver.

He put a comforting arm around her shoulders and looked past her to the window of the backdoor. "*Dhyoeg mri egow!*" he whispered as he released her. A strong feeling of *déjà vous* fell over him from the day on the back porch when Hiram witnessed his inadvertent tearing of Sophia's sleeve from her dress.

"What did you say?" Livia asked, wiping a stray tear from her cheek.

Rahzvon choked out the words "He sees us; he is watching from the kitchen window."

Livia turned, seeing no one there. "Who?"

"Hiram."

She looked up nervously to Rahzvon. They turned toward the back door, preparing for the moment when Hiram would exit.

"I would suggest that we go inside, but...it is too late," Rahzvon stammered. His hands began to sweat beneath the thin bandages.

"You shan't worry; Hiram would never strike a defenseless man and you *did* save Sophia."

"You are referring to a man who may be involved in a heinous crime."

"Oh, *Rahzvon*, please stop." She stood tall, still holding Rahzvon's arm. They stood silently like a pair of scared rabbits waiting in a hole for the fox above them to appear.

As the heavy cloud of doubt of Hiram's innocence in the alleged crime crept over them, they walked casually toward the door.

"Livia, has Hiram ever said anything that would make you question his character?" Rahzvon whispered.

"Something to make me think that he was capable of holding someone—?" She stopped suddenly and tightened her grip on Rahzvon's arm.

"What? Tell me."

"No, no, he was only teasing me."

"What, Livia? Quickly, what did he say?"

"Well, he said that he often wished that he could keep me in a cage, safe from the world. But I am sure it was only in jest."

Rahzvon's eyes widened; his heart began to pound. He took Livia by the shoulders. "Promise me that you will not let on that you suspect him of anything. You may jeopardize your safety."

"Rahzvon, I love him, I cannot do this!" she said through clenched teeth. The door opened. Hiram stepped onto the porch.

Rahzvon responded in record speed with his cover story, "Sir, please explain to Miss Nichols that you approve—that she may continue with the plans for the play-yard—that you really do *not* have any objection."

Hiram did not respond.

Livia wavered in the silence. "Rahzvon, you need not defend me; it is *his* home and his estate," she added to the charade.

Rahzvon slipped his supporting arm from her shoulders. "Reassure her, Hiram," he said confidently.

Hiram's condemning gaze flashed from Rahzvon to Livia several times. "Whatever you desire, Livy," he stated sharply. He went inside.

Livia's shoulders relaxed; Rahzvon drew a deep breath of relief.

"Let him go, Livia. As long as he is angry, you can keep your distance, hiding your suspicion of his involvement with Avera. At least until we clarify his guilt."

"Innocence!"

"Do you actually believe that Hiram is totally incapable of such an atrocity? At times, Even though I admire and respect him, I dare say that I fear him. He has a mysterious side that I cannot fathom, nor care to."

"Are you insinuating that Hiram has a dark side? I take offense. Yes, he is reserved at times and animated at others, but mysterious, he is not."

"*Animated?*"

"I know him better than anyone, and I can

assure you that Hiram is not the McDonnally responsible for that woman's ill-fate."

"That remains to be verified."

They left the garden; Livia entered the house where she found Hiram standing in the hall and apparently deep in thought.

"Hiram, about Rahzvon—"

"Your business discussions with Mr. Sierzik are of no interest to me."

She stepped closer. "Are you angry with me?" she asked timidly.

"Nay, not with you."

"Surely, not with Rahzvon. He has assisted me in so many ways."

Hiram raised a brow.

"Shame on you!" she scorned.

Hiram offered a forgiving grin and pulled her next to him. "You are too bonnie for me lassie. No matter how irrational, seeing you with any man... draws out the green-eyed monster." He took her hand. "Livia Nichols, there is only one way to deal with a beauty such as you."

Livia bit her bottom lip and looked nervously to his hand tight on her waist.

"I should have to build our house on Duncan Ridge, surround you with objects of grandeur, lock the door, and throw away the key. Your beauty shall be for my eyes only."

Goosebumps crept up her arms.

He leaned down to kiss her, but she slid away, avoiding his advances.

"What is this? You refuse me, Livy?"

"No...I just remembered I have to place the order with Dagmar for the miniature stove set to insure its arrival before Parents' Night. I will see you later!" She ran to the hall to find the servant, Roy.

In the meantime, Rahzvon went to the Zigmann cottage to find Sophia, where he found Guillaume sketching on the porch.

"What are you drawing, Zigmann?" He asked with frustration, assuming they were plans for Sophia's nursery in the mansion.

"Designs for a timber-clad house."

Rahzvon glanced down at the sketch. "Timber-clad? It looks like a hunting lodge."

"It is a new concept for homes."

"Guillaume, is Phia inside?"

"No, she went for a walk with Allison."

"Zigmann, you read the note that I had you take from my pocket."

Guillaume stopped drawing and looked up. "Is that a question?"

"There is no time for games. Confess, now."

"Very well, yes, I did." He laid down his drawing implements. "Who is this woman, Avera S. and *which* McDonnally is the scoundrel?" he asked with the interest of the village gossip.

"Zigmann, you have to swear that you won't breath a word of this to anyone. Or is it too late?"

Guillaume raised his right hand, "I swear, I spoke to no one about it—not Allison, not anyone."

"I will honor your word, but you had better be telling the truth." Rahzvon sat down on the step next to him. "I found the note tacked beneath the table in our cottage."

"Really? Is it not most fortunate that your table hung from the ceiling, allowing you to find it? Clever wife of yours."

"Never mind that. Only one other person,

other than the two of us...eh, and one child, knows about this."

"Is Avera the child?"

"No, Zigmann." Rahzvon rolled his eyes. "Livia and Marvel Wheaton."

"Little Marvel Wheaton? She knows about this and you were concerned about *my* integrity?"

"*Zigmann.*"

"I had no idea that Marvel and Livia were confidants. Naomi and Marvel, perhaps—"

"Zigmann, they are not! That is not pertinent!" Rahzvon got control, "Now listen to me. Livia is sworn to secrecy; Marvel is another matter. The point is that the author of this note may need my help. This is serious!"

Guillaume gave a little chuckle.

"Do you find this to be amusing?" Rahzvon scorned.

"No...no, it is just that you sound like Sophia. They say that when people are together for—"

"If my hands were completely healed," Rahzvon threatened.

"Sorry." Guillaume leaned toward Rahzvon and asked, "Do you believe the guilty party is one of the wealthiest, most powerful men in the country?"

"I don't know what to believe. As much as I detest the man at times, I cannot imagine Hiram capable of such abominable behavior."

"*Edward* is certainly not suspect. Now, Hiram's father—I have my doubts about him. We need more information. We need a time-frame." He placed his sketches in the leather valise. "Come along, we need to find out who resided in the cottage prior to your possession." Guillaume got up and tossed his valise inside the front door.

"Zigmann, what are you doing?"

"We are going to visit the authority, Mr. Kilvert, the postman."

"I do not remember inviting you to join in this investigation."

"Rahzvon, you need my help. Neither you, nor Livia, know enough about the village and the residents in order to proceed with a thorough investigation. I do. I will get a carriage, since horseback is not an option for you."

Rahzvon breathed a resigned sigh and followed him.

When they reached the Kilvert cottage, Mr. Kilvert was leaning on the front porch column, sipping a drink.

"Afternoon, Guillaume, Rahzvon."

"Good afternoon, Mr. Kilvert. Enjoying a day out of the saddle?" Guillaume asked.

"Aye. Rahzvon, how are yer hands?"

"Healing, thank you. Has Jake left yet, to serve?"

"Aye. 'Tis a good thing ye tied the knot wit' Miss Sophia."

Rahzvon hesitated uncomfortably believing that Mr. Kilvert was insinuating the *need* to marry Sophia. "Sir?"

"Me son Jake's fiancée was a wee taken wit' ye," he said with narrowed eyes.

"Agnes, taken with Rahzvon?" Astounded, Guillaume turned to Rahzvon.

"Aye," Mr. Kilvert continued, "she nearly broke off the engagement, frettin' o'er the likes of ye." He squinted at Rahzvon. Rahzvon forced a grin and looked away.

"Agnes, taken with Rahzvon? I cannot believe

it. Who would have thought that—?"

"*Zigmann.*" Rahzvon gave him a sharp kick to his ankle.

Guillaume grimaced then got back to the matter at hand. "About our visit, today, sir. As you know, the Sierziks resided at the little cottage outside the village."

"Guillaume, I *am* the postman. Wee place; can understand yer movin' out. I was in it, but once before ye moved in, but I shall ne'er forget it. Aye, ne'er saw so many useless things crammed into one cottage in all me life—hundreds o' pieces of porcelain, everywhere." He took another drink.

Guillaume continued, "Yes, well, as there were a few things left behind by the prior residents— things that Sophia wants, Rahzvon would like to do the right thing and purchase them from...from the residents that left them."

Rahzvon was amazed by Guillaume's quick thinking, but realized that Guillaume, a noted stumblebum, had more experience "thinking on his feet" than the average individual did.

"If they didna want them, why purchase them?" Mr. Kilvert asked suspiciously.

Guillaume looked to Rahzvon for an answer and then put an arm over Rahzvon's shoulder. "My friend, here, is a superstitious man—common to the Kosdrevan culture." Rahzvon's jaws tightened at the derogatory connotation. Guillaume smiled. "Yes, the Kosdrevians feel that evil spirits can follow you, if items are taken without having been properly purchased."

"Hmm?" Mr. Kilvert looked at the handsome young Rahzvon with a disturbed expression." He sat down his drink on the porch rail. "'Twas the widow McNewell and her charge."

"Her charge?" Rahzvon asked.

"Aye, a young woman—a stranger to the moors. She ne'er left the cottage, inflicted wit' an infirmity."

"She was ill?" Guillaume eagerly cut in.

Mr. Kilvert leaned forward. "I'm not one to gossip. Her ailment was in the head. Many o' the villagers said they heard her screamin', tryin' to escape."

Guillaume grabbed Rahzvon's forearm, which Rahzvon jerked from his panicking grasp.

Mr. Kilvert broke the silence, "Ye ne'er saw her ghost did ye? I hear tell the lassie passed on there, but there werena witnesses," he whispered.

Rahzvon swallowed hard, "Do you know where Mrs. McNewell is living, Mr. Kilvert?"

"Aye. She lives in Devonshire, near the border. Her sickly sister lives there wit' her."

"Thank you, sir. When you write Jake, please tell him that we send our best wishes for his safety," Rahzvon said, starting to leave.

"Aye. He's at the London Aerodrome, now, waitin' for orders."

"Thank you again, Mr. Kilvert," Rahzvon said, nudging Guillaume. "How far is it to Devonshire?" he asked in a low tone.

"About an hour. Good afternoon, Mr. Kilvert!" Guillaume called as they climbed into the cart.

"Let's go, Zigmann."

At McDonnally Manor, Livia, still disturbed by Hiram's second remark regarding her future confinement, paced in the parlor. He would be returning soon. Preoccupied with his possible involvement with Avera, Livia wandered aimlessly, incapable of attacking her mounds of schoolwork.

"Miss Nichols, may I bring you some tea or cookies, er...biscuits?" the servant asked.

Livia laughed. "Hello Roy. No, thank you. Still having trouble with the language difference?" She smiled.

"I admit that it is tough at times. I have to admit that I was very embarrassed when Mr. McDonnally asked me for the torch the other evening. Albert found me constructing one from and old broom handle and rags and informed me that the flashlight in his hand *was* the torch."

Livia giggled. "Other than the communication difficulties, how do you like Scotland?"

"It really is quite similar to Virginia in its landscape...without the castles."

"Yes, it is somewhat of a fairytale atmosphere."

"Now the culture, well that takes some getting used to; a tea every time that you turn around," Roy added.

"It grows on you after you have been here for awhile."

They turned to the window to Rusty's barking in the drive.

Livia stepped over and looked out. "That must be Hiram returning."

"And that reminds me, I have orders to 'remove the dampers from the dustbin before Rusty pinches them'—whatever they are."

"Flat cakes," Livia explained, laughing. "It *is* nice having another American to chat with. Good day, Roy."

Yes, Ma'am. I mean, aye, Mum." Roy grinned and left to continue his chores, elsewhere.

Livia moved slowly into the hall and peered toward the back door. Hiram entered and went directly to the kitchen. She continued down the corridor and approached him, trying to maintain a clear head and an open mind to the Avera mystery.

"Hello, love," Hiram greeted her, drying his hands.

"I will fetch Eloise and tell her that you are ready for tea."

"Wait, I nearly forgot," he said, grinning and reached into his pocket.

Livia's eyes nearly popped from her head at the rusty pair of handcuffs.

"The Fletcher lad gave me these in return for rescuing his piglet, Forbes." Hiram stood looming over Livia and ran his fingers through her tresses, trying not to touch her with his filthy clothes. "Now, my bonnie lass, these will be quite useful, in detaining you, the next time you attempt to run away from me." He threw back his head and laughed.

Livia, seeing no humor in the condemning comment, stood motionless.

An hour later, Rahzvon and Guillaume were heading down the road in the direction of Lochmoor Glen.

"How are you going to explain your absence to Sophia? Do you realize how long we have been gone?" Guillaume asked.

Rahzvon ignored his inquiries and solemnly pondered the outcome of their visit to Devonshire.

"Rahzvon?"

"I wish that I would have never found that blasted note."

"'Tis a sticky wicket. Did you see the widow McNewell's face when we mentioned Avera? I thought that I was going to have to pick up her eyes from the floor. Grief-stricken, she was not. She was hiding something; she not so much as asked our names, let alone, invited us in. Why would she ask when we saw Avera last, if Avera passed on in the cottage?"

"I got the impression that Avera is very much alive and Mrs. McNewell believes that we may have information to the woman's whereabouts. I can just about guarantee that Mrs. McNewell is desperate to find her, too."

"You think that Avera escaped?"

"I would bet on it."

They were about three miles from Devonshire, when Guillaume and Rahzvon noticed that a rider was shadowing them. Finally, the stranger rode up alongside of their cart. Guillaume halted their horses.

The man addressed them, "Mrs. McNewell desires a second meeting wit' ye."

Rahzvon glanced curiously at Guillaume, "When?"

"Directly."

Rahzvon nodded and Guillaume turned the horses to follow the messenger back to Devonshire.

Rahzvon nudged Guillaume. "She has had second thoughts. We were too valuable, to let us go. I knew that she was desperate for information."

"As are we," Guillaume added.

Chapter 11

"Gwynn"

"If from that great, unselfish stream,
The Golden Rule we drink,
We'll keep God's laws, and have no cause
To say 'I didn't think'."

—Ella Wheeler Wilcox

Once again, the disturbingly gaunt individual by the name of Mr. Sickby invited Rahzvon and Guillaume into the residence of Mrs. McNewell. However, on this occasion the young men were asked to wait in the drawing room. The house was bursting at the seams with antique bric and brac; porcelain figurines of every size imaginable shrouded every inch of every table and shelf. Paintings, sketches, crewel and embroidered tapestries plastered the walls. The eclectic home resembled a curio shop rather than a private residence. The young men stood in awe, noting the similarity to the postman's description of the cottage.

"Please, sit," Mr. Sickby requested.

They looked to the pillow-laden couch and began rearranging the bolster and assorted toss pillows, in order to make adequate room to sit. As there was no room to lay the pillows, other than the floor, each held three on their lap and waited for the arrival of their hostess.

Instead, a stringy, thin creature appeared, struggling to balance a refreshment tray. Guillaume and Rahzvon awkwardly managed to stand at her entry. Apparently baffled by their courtesy, she paused and reiterated the instruction to take their seats. Her waif-like appearance concerned the men. Seemingly beckoning for their assistance in something of unknown origin, her sunken eyes rested heavily upon theirs. She did not speak. They offered their gratitude and took care to lift the teacups from her bony fingers. Guillaume and Rahzvon thanked her and rested their saucers on the pillows on their laps. She stood over them, looking as if she was about to say something, but withdrew instantly at

Mrs. McNewell's entry. Being a large, rotund woman, who was obviously well fed, Mrs. McNewell was a visual opposite of her servant.

"Gentlemen." They attempted to rise again when Mrs. McNewell stopped them. "Dunna bother. So ye hae heard o' the lass in me charge?"

Rahzvon replied, "Yes, the postman informed us that at one time, you shared the cottage with her."

"Kilvert, eh?" She peered over the top of her spectacles. "These things that ye wanted to purchase from me—describe them."

Every muscle tightened in Rahzvon's body. He looked quickly to Guillaume for assistance, "What were they called?"

Guillaume shrugged.

Rahzvon cleared his throat. "Mrs. McNewell, I need to explain something about myself."

She squinted skeptically.

Rahzvon gripped the teacup with both hands. "I am not a Scot."

"That doesna surprise me."

"Actually, I am a Kosdrevian...from Kosdrev. Although I speak English better than the average Kosdrevian, with English being my second language...well, there are many terms of which I am not familiar. In Kosdrev, we would call them *dith gustipi*. My wife would know what they are in English."

"Yer wife? Is she a Kos—whatever, as well?" Mrs. McNewell stood tapping her index finger on the mantle.

"No, she is a returning Scot." Rahzvon hesitated then clarified, "She is waiting for me at McDonnally Manor."

Mrs. McNewell's hand immediately shot

across the mantle sending a dozen statuettes to the hearth. The quick movement and sudden crash startled all three. Wide-eyed, Rahzvon and Guillaume observed the thousand pieces at her feet.

"Gwynn, fetch the broom and dustbin!" their hostess shouted.

The spindly housekeeper returned toting a broom, which looked too large for her to manipulate. She did her best to make a hasty clean up, making occasional eye contact with the guests.

"Hurry up, Gwynn! One would never believe we're from the same stock."

Same stock? Both men were appalled that Gwynn may be the sister, who Mr. Kilvert had mentioned. Gwynn rushed from the room

"What is yer name, lad?" Mrs. McNewell asked.

Rahzvon hesitated, and then replied utilizing the name he used in Kosdrev and his father's middle name, "Marcus, Marcus Ormand."

"And I ask what business would yer wife be havin' at the McDonnally estate?"

"We live there now; we moved from the cottage."

"Servants, are ye?"

"No."

She grinned sinisterly, "Ye need to be doin' better than that, lad. The McDonnallys takin' boarders? They could purchase most o' Scotland. They wouldna be lettin' their rooms."

"I never said that we were boarders," Rahzvon said coolly.

"Nay?"

"My wife is of the McDonnally clan."

Mrs. McNewell froze. Guillaume and Rahzvon studied her reaction. She then took a turn about the room. "Did Master McDonnally send ye?"

"No, Madame, we came at *your* request."

She spun around, nearly knocking over a Duncan Phyfe end table, loaded with salt and pepper sets.

"Dunna be insolent wit' me, lad! I am referrin' to your first visit."

Rahzvon lifted his cup with his bandaged fingers and confidently pretended to take a sip, considering the tea may be laced with some harmful ingredient. He then replied nonchalantly, "No."

Guillaume took the cue to taste his, but Rahzvon's sharp elbow deterred him. "Ahh!" Guillaume quickly dabbed the spilled tea from the crocheted pillow. "Sorry, my hand slipped."

"Gwynn! Get back here!" the widow called.

Gwynn quickly removed the soiled pillow and again summoned the guests' attention with a concerned gaze before leaving the room.

Mrs. McNewell wiped her hands on her skirt. "How did ye injure yer hands?" she asked.

"A fire at the McDonnally mansion."

"A fire?" Her brows knitted. She walked to the window and then turned, glaring at Rahzvon and then Guillaume.

"Who would ye be?" she demanded.

Guillaume smiled, "Robin Hood."

The widow scowled.

Guillaume quickly interjected, "That is H-u-i-d. My parents were avid readers of—"

"I hae no recollection o' leavin' anythin' at the cottage. Mr. Ormand, tell yer wife that the items are free o' charge."

"Thank you is there anything else?" Rahzvon asked suggestively.

"Nay, 'tis good ye returned, I willna be here after today." She escorted them to the door. "Good day," she said, frowning anxiously before closing the door.

"We need to speak with Gwynn," Rahzvon said as they walked to the carriage. "Unconscionable the way that woman treats her sister."

Guillaume glanced back at the house. Then he saw her. "Gwynn is in the upstairs window." He turned back. "I think that she is motioning for us to go to the well."

"Keep walking, *Robin*. Drive the carriage up the street. Once we are out of view, I will slip back to the well."

Rahzvon moved stealthily through the cemetery in the adjacent lot. He could see Gwynn in the distance, standing at the back corner of the house. He checked the windows—no spectators. He dashed toward the well. Gwynn peeked from behind the corner of the house and quickly joined him. She raised the bucket, ladled out a scoop and lifted it to Rahzvon's mouth. Her voice trembled, as she spoke. She, then, vanished behind the house. Rahzvon wiped his mouth with the corner of his shirtsleeve and ran back to the carriage. He jumped up next to Guillaume, "Drive on, Zigmann."

"Did you see her? What did she say? Tell me, man, tell me!"

"She said 'Avera escaped and Mr. McDonnally is in grave danger. You must warn him.'"

"I must?" Guillaume asked with alarm.

"*No*, Zigmann. She meant you and me; that

we must warn him."

"Danger from what?"

"Avera's wrath, I suspect."

"Which McDonnally? Did she say?"

"No."

"We have to warn both of them?"

"Yes and by warning both or either of them, we will be confirming our knowledge of the crime," Rahzvon said, shaking his head.

"A pickle, Rahzvon, we are in a blasted pickle."

"I know," he replied with despair. "Let's go Zigmann."

In his study, Hiram toiled over dozens of IOU's that Livia had acquired for her students' tuition. After a futile attempt to organize them, he thrust them back into the basket and painstakingly dealt with them one at a time.

Meanwhile, in the large common room in the west wing, which Hiram so generously donated for Livia's School of Little Dreams, Livia, anxious about Hiram's questionable remarks involving the handcuffs and her confinement, busied herself with a school art project. She had counted out three pieces of straw to become the whiskers for each child's cat picture and placed them next to the bean "eyes." After cutting the yarn pieces for the tails, she began cutting the ears from a black piece of leather, when she heard a sound in the storeroom.

"Rusty? Is that you?" she called out to the Zigmann's mischievous little dachshund. "Come here, boy!" she called, trying to keep count. The dog had been fascinated with the art supplies, so Livia was certain that he had discovered the box of yarn that she failed to cover on the lower shelf. Another sudden crash in the backroom startled her. With her nerves, already frayed, she mumbled in frustration. "Oh, now see what you have done, I have lost count." She put down the scissors and went to review the damage.

In that the storeroom was quite dark, Livia opened the door wider, offering a stream of light from the adjoining room. She slid her feet to avoid stepping on the perpetrator. "Rusty?"

As fate would have it, taking the next three steps would be the last thing that Livia Nichols would remember for the next hour.

Hiram, now, sat with his feet propped upon his desk, and stroked his beard in the usual manner while deep in thought.

"Why, in the name of all that is rational, did I offer my services?" He glared at the detestable basket of paper scraps, wondering how it was possible that Livia had accrued such a multitude in such a short time. His recordings nearly filled the ledger pages. However, over half were marked out and rewritten under different headings. He pulled his feet down and slammed the ledger closed. "Enough of this. I am hiring a full-time accountant for her."

He left his study in search of his twin, Hannah, who he found in the parlor, chatting with his niece, Sophia.

"Hiram, did you know that Agnes Murray has gone to Greenwich to work at the ammunition factory?" Hannah asked.

"The Royal Ordinance?"

"Yes, they are employing thousands of women," Sophia chimed in.

"Is this commentary directed to my abstinence from involvement with the military?" Hiram demanded.

"No brother. Of course not, your work at the farms is quite sufficient and admirable."

Hiram's brows knitted. "Has Mr. Raheleka mentioned the duration of his visit?"

"No, why do you ask?"

"I need his assistance in procuring an accountant for Livy. Her bookkeeping is less than desirable." He sat down in the overstuffed chair and closed his eyes, and rubbed his forehead. "Nay, it is a *disaster* and I have not the time."

"Brother, you look exhausted. Please, go take a nap until dinner, if only for an hour."

"Yes, Uncle, you look positively horrid." Sophia shook her head.

"Mrs. Sierzik, you would not be looking your best had you stayed up all night for the foaling of Mrs. Cassaway's mare," Hiram spoke in his defense.

Sophia laid down the questionable product of her attempt at knitting. "Well, horses may have their babies at dawn, but I shall not. I shall do all that I can to wait until mid-afternoon, so that I have had a full night's sleep. I intend to look beautiful the first minute my daughter sees me."

Hiram listened with a perplexed look and shook his head, "You are right; none of this is making sense—I need some sleep. Good afternoon, ladies." He dragged himself from the chair and slowly left the room.

"Sophia, as your mother, I should tell you, that giving birth is not that simple."

Sophia moved next to Hannah. "Mother tell

me about the day when I was born. It has been years since I heard the story."

"Very well. It was a cold fall day. Your father and I were preparing the café for the grand opening. I remember that I was very angry. I had ordered blue tablecloths, but had received red ones. I was *furious*."

"Because it was the *Café de Bleu*."

"Exactly. I had one last parcel to open, which revealed only more of the same. Red dinner napkins. Now, I was seeing *red* beyond the linens. I snatched up the purchase order and marched, well, waddled in a huff down to the shipping office."

"Did my father go with you?"

"No. He said nothing and went about hooking up the stove."

"What happened at the shipping office? Did they have your order there?"

"Actually, it was quite a distance from the café, so my temper had reached its limit by the time that I entered the office. The clerk was a snippy, old man who made a practice of ignoring dissatisfied customers. I wasted no time in demanding that he check the storeroom for my packages with the blue linens."

"Did he?"

"Of course not. He would have thrown me out, had I not been in that condition." Hannah started to laugh, "Oh, Sophia, I wish that you could have been there. That is right; you were there!"

Sophia laughed with her. "Go on, Mother."

"My dear, I was stark raving mad. Imagine this: the tiny room strewn with torn brown paper, parcel strings, purchases ranging from sabers to ladies undergarments and lying in the center of it all on two woolen blankets imported from—"

Hannah stopped smiling. She stared at her daughter and shuddered as a chill ran through her body.

"Mother, what is wrong? Have you taken ill?" Sophia put a hand on Hannah's shoulder.

Hannah reached up and laid her hand on Sophia's.

"Sophia, I cannot believe it. It is the first time I thought about it."

"Believe what, Mother?" Sophia asked anxiously.

"I knew that the name was familiar, but I could not place it."

"*Mother!*"

"Sophia, brace yourself. 'Tis very odd, but true."

"What, Mama, what?"

"The woolen blankets, Sophia, that I delivered on, were imported from Kosdrev."

Sophia's dark McDonnally eyes widened as they met her mother's. There was a moment of silence.

"Are you sure, Mother? How did you know? Was there a label?" Sophia asked, moving to the edge of the seat.

"No, but an irate, scholarly man entered the office directly after you were born. Yes, he was outraged. I would have never known from where they were imported, if he had not arrived, protesting. He was shouting '*Non, non pas mes couvertures de Kosdrev*'."

"No, no, not my blankets from Kosdrev? Oh, Mother, my meeting with Rahzvon was planned from the day that I was born," Sophia said with awe. She smiled and placed her hands on her belly, when Rahzvon and Guillaume appeared in the archway.

"Where is Hiram?" Rahzvon asked impatiently.

Sophia ran to him. "No hello kiss? You shan't believe what I have to tell you," she said, beaming. "We were destined to be together. Are you not curious as to why I know this?"

"Phia! This is urgent! Where is your uncle?"

Hannah's smile faded to concern. "He has gone to his bedchamber to nap."

Rahzvon shot out of the room and sprinted up the stairs. He pounded on the door.

"Rahzvon!" Sophia called after him and stomped her foot.

Guillaume remained to console the women, but refused to offer any information, despite their prodding.

"What the devil is going on?" Hiram left his bed and opened the door.

"Sir, I have to speak with you. It is urgent," Rahzvon insisted.

"Sophia?" he asked with alarm.

"No, no she is fine," Rahzvon reassured.

"Come in and close the door. Please do not tell me that this concerns issues of livestock."

"No, sir."

"Then what? I refuse to discuss any topic concerning Livy, including enlarging her school," Hiram warned.

"No, sir, this has nothing to do with Livia."

"Well, speak up, lad. Why in the blazes did you waken me?"

Rahzvon hesitated and glanced around the room. "I do not know where to begin."

"Mr. Sierzik, if you do not *begin* immediately, I shall have you thrown out of my house and your marriage annulled."

"Yes, sir. Please, sit down."

Hiram stepped into his face, "Rahzvon, I am warning you."

"The cottage—Phia's and mine. It had a note hanging from the ceiling—I mean the table—you are in danger, sir," Rahzvon said with desperation.

Hiram squinted with confusion, stepped back, and dropped down to the bed. "Do I appear to be a man in good humor prepared to solve riddles?"

"No, sir. I found a note attached beneath the table in the cottage."

"And why in heaven's name should this concern me?" Hiram said wearily.

"Because, because it had your name on it."

"Hiram stood up. "I do not know what kind of game you are engaged in, but you had better leave, now, before you find yourself on the first floor."

"You have to listen to me, Hiram."

"I never wrote any confounded note, much less pasted it on your blasted hanging furniture!"

"Sir, I am aware of that fact. The note was authored by a woman, named Avera."

Hiram was silent. His face grew dark. He closed his eyes and grimaced. Rahzvon stepped fearfully back, praying that Hiram would consider Sophia before retaliating.

Hiram stepped away and moved to the other side of the room, facing the drape-covered window.

It is him. He knows what I am talking about, Rahzvon thought and stepped nervously back to the door. "Sir, in the note, she claimed that one of the McDonnally men had held her captive there."

Hiram's fists tightened. He drew a deep breath

and turned to face Rahzvon, and grabbed hold of the bedpost. "I knew it was not over." He walked over to the other side of the bed, and sat down. "I need to explain." He nervously rubbed his hand across his bearded chin. "The year before I left Switzerland to return home, a young woman met me at the park down the street from the clock shop. After a few casual meetings, she made claim to be my missing twin, Hannah. Being an infant at the time of my sister's kidnapping, I had never seen Hannah as an adult. Initially, I considered the possibility, as the woman did share many of the McDonnally characteristics in her appearance—the eyes, hair, stature. After a brief evaluation, I paid an investigator to check into her past. He, of course, quickly discovered that she was an imposter and merely seeking Hannah's fortune and mine. He refused to reveal her identity, as I would not compensate him for that information. However, it left me concerned and baffled. Although it was public knowledge of my sister's disappearance, I had no idea as to how she discovered that I was a McDonnally. I had kept my identity discreet and lived under the assumed name of Jack Rands for many years."

"What did you do?"

"I confronted her."

Chapter 111

"The Message"

"As a moth gnaws a garment,
So does envy consume a man."

—St. John Chrysostom

Hiram continued his explanation to Rahzvon, "I told her that her story was of no interest to me, as I was not a member of the McDonnally clan. My denial infuriated her and within no time, she was blackmailing me, planning to go public with my true identity. Determined to remain out of the public eye, like a fool, I gave her most of my savings. This did not stop her. She returned for more. As I did not have access to my inheritance, she began intimidating me with threats to my family members, if I did not continue to pay her. She became erratic and dangerous. I left Switzerland immediately, reclaimed my position in the clan."

Hiram took a breath. "Obviously, it had not ended there. Her obsession for the money, evolved into a consuming hatred and...well I can only assume that those who I paid to keep her out of Britain have duped me." Hiram stood and gave a brief nod. "So, she was held in the cottage—confined from further blackmailing me, but in Scotland, nonetheless. I can only assume that those I hired kept her in close proximity with hopes of an opportunity to blackmail me, as well. I was told that she was institutionalized and later, that she had passed on."

"Hiram," Rahzvon approached him, "she is very much alive, and has escaped."

"Escaped? So that was why blackmail was no longer an option."

"Sir, today, I spoke with Mrs. McNewell, the woman who kept Avera in the cottage. Afterward, Mrs. McNewell's sister discreetly confided that Avera had not only escaped, but was determined to get revenge. She insisted that I warn you. At the time, I did not know which Mr. McDonnally."

"Revenge, eh? Nay, Edward knows nothing of this," he mumbled. His thoughts fled back to Avera's threats to destroy his home, his family, his 'perfect face,' and to end his life. He threw his head back, clutched it within his hands, and let out a sigh of despair.

"What can I do to help?"

"Keep a close eye on Sophia and Hannah for the next few days, but tell them nothing. We do not want to alarm Sophia. I shall make the necessary arrangements to have this woman apprehended, as quickly as possible."

"What about you? Perhaps, you should hire someone to—"

"To look after me? Nay, I can take care of myself. However, she has threatened to destroy this house. I will alert the servants and the grounds men to keep a twenty-four hour watch until she is found."

"What about Livia? Are you going to tell her? She *is* responsible for the children at the school."

"I shall inform her directly. Has she returned from the west wing?"

"I have not seen her."

Hiram pulled on his boots and slipped on his jacket. "Does anyone else know about this?"

Rahzvon dreaded this inquiry, knowing Hiram's opinion of Guillaume. He replied reluctantly, "Yes."

"Who?"

"Zigmann—Guillaume."

"Guillaume! Man, are you daft? Granted, we all like Guillaume, but whatever possessed you to confide in that half-wit?"

"Begging your pardon, sir, but he did save Sophia's life," Rahzvon said, following Hiram into the hall.

"Sophia's?"

"Yes, from the drunkards, when we were en route to Eyemou—" Rahzvon paused realizing this was only another report that would condemn him, as Hiram had objected to Sophia's accompaniment to Kosdrev. "Sir, Zigmann, found out about the note, purely by accident, but he accompanied me to speak to Mrs. McNewell about Avera."

"Avera," Hiram muttered, moving swiftly toward the staircase where they encountered Sophia.

She demanded, "Tell me this urgent news, this minute!"

"If it concerned you, my dear, I would," Hiram said, slipping past her. He entered the parlor, "Hannah, have you seen Livy?"

"No, not of late."

Hiram moved back into the hall, snagging a hold on Guillaume's arm and dragging him into the dining room. Curious as she was, Sophia remained behind.

"Sir, I promise, my lips are sealed," Guillaume said, panicking.

"Zigmann, your silence is not all that I require. Keep a close eye on the cottage, your parents, and Allison. Do you understand?"

"You can count on me, sir."

Hiram raised his brows, sighed and replied, "Good." He released Guillaume's arm and rushed to the west wing to speak with Livia. "Dear God, why could you not spare me this intrusion?" Hiram questioned if he already had enough with which to contend, as he entered the common room of Livia's school.

"Livy?"

He stepped next to her desk, noting the prototype of her cat project and smiled. "You creative little lass," he mumbled. "Livy!" he called.

The rooms were quiet. He walked to the window. *Where are you?* A cold shiver crept over him. Something was not right. He moved quickly toward the kitchen and back through the common room, when a fearful eeriness encompassed him. His steps quickened toward the storeroom. He pushed open the door. He could not breathe. The room was a shambles; toys and supplies scattered around the floor—crushed baskets throughout.

He picked up one of the demolished baskets and carried it into the light. *What has happened here?* He dropped it in horror. The bloodstained basket lay at his feet.

"Livy!" he bellowed. He looked anxiously toward the door; there the mystery ended. Scrolled across the chalkboard were the horrifying words that lacerated his heart, now pounding heavily in his chest.

> *You stole my life—for that*
> *I have stolen yours.*
> *Avera*

"Nay! Livy!"

His tormented cry heard throughout the mansion, sent his family and staff running to the west wing. There they found the desk overturned, and Hiram staring at the cryptic message, clutching Livia's art project to his chest, and tears streaming down his face. Rahzvon instantly felt Hiram's pain in reading the shocking words. "No...no."

"Uncle Hiram! What has happened?" Sophia

screamed. She began weeping hysterically when he did not respond from his trance-like state.

"Phia, he will be fine!" Rahzvon said, turning to Hannah and Eloise. "Get her out of here!"

They hastily removed Sophia from the scene.

"Get a hold, Hiram. Come on, we have to find Livia," Rahzvon insisted.

Hiram remained motionless. Rahzvon had never seen Hiram so affected. Tearing a room apart, yes—but never catatonic.

"Do it man, or I shall!" Guillaume commanded.

Rahzvon looked anxiously to Guillaume and then turned to Hiram. "*Fivdom greog,*" he mumbled before his hand met the side of Hiram's face with stinging force. This selfless action successfully brought Hiram back to reality.

"Hiram, there is no time to waste, we have to search for Livia," Rahzvon said, grabbing Hiram's arm. Hiram stared at the cat picture, folded it, and placed it in his jacket pocket. Rahzvon spoke gently, "We will find her and bring her safely home."

Hiram's lips trembled as he looked down at the bloodstained basket. Rahzvon's gaze followed; he closed his eyes with the unbearable thought that they may have lost Livia forever.

Rahzvon shook Hiram by the shoulders, "No! No, Hiram, do not believe it. We will find her."

Guillaume, skeptical, sadly shook his head, but added, "We shall."

Hiram wiped his eyes. "Aye, she has probably taken Livia from the estate."

Rahzvon agreed, "Yes, but we will first search the grounds—the barn—the garden—everywhere. Zigmann, notify the grounds men and inquire if anyone has seen a carriage or riders leave the estate."

"Directly." Guillaume shot down the hall.

"Rahzvon, come with me, we will search the perimeter, including Duncan Ridge," Hiram instructed.

The search continued until nightfall. Livia's kidnapping became common knowledge to all of Lochmoor Glen and the residents joined willingly in the search.

Hiram sat in the parlor surrounded by the volunteers who were exhausted and emotionally devastated at their failure to discover information of Livia's disappearance. His weary body was aching; his heart agonizing. His thoughts fell back to the time when he was held prisoner and left to die and then to Avera, captive in the cottage. He had to find Livia, alive and well. Every building, barn and woods had been searched, and yet there was no sign or witness to the departure of Livia and her captor. Frustration and confusion were eminent.

"People do not vanish as specters in a dream," Hiram muttered.

Edward sat next to his nephew and placed an arm over Hiram's shoulders. "Hiram, you need to rest. We cannot search in the dark. We will meet here again at dawn."

Hiram raised his head. "How can I sleep, not knowing...?"

"Have faith," Naomi said, standing in the archway.

"Come along," Edward said, giving Hiram's shoulders a squeeze. "She will probably soon contact us for a ransom. Livia is fine."

Hiram offered a few words of his gratitude to the remaining neighbors and slowly ascended the stairs to his bedchamber.

Livia's eyes opened slowly. Her vision was slightly blurred and her head throbbing. She felt the burning of the corners of her mouth from the tight cloth gag restraint. Her wrists were sore from the tight ropes that bound them. She tried to focus on the woman's face before her.

"Strange, waking in an unknown place, to an unknown future, to an unfamiliar face, eh? Yes, Livia Nichols, I have all the answers." The woman smiled sinisterly and began the unsavory explanation.

"Why you ask? Because your precious Mr. McDonnally is a greedy miser—an ogre who has no value for human life. He will soon see that his pretty face and all his tainted money are of little value in rescuing you from your fate. Nothing directed to you, personally, Livia. I understand that you were acquainted with my stepsister, Delilah."

Delilah? Livia was unaware that the owner of the Switzerland clock shop had another daughter, stepchild or otherwise. Delilah had never mentioned her.

"Surprised, Livia?" She stood up and walked over to where Rusty, the little dachshund, lay quietly on a pile of rags. Livia noted that he, like her, was gagged and bound. Her heart went out to him.

"Little devil. I did not count on him being here, but I couldn't do him in. Most animals are better than people." The woman wrung her hands.

"Yes, Livia, Delilah is my sister. She and I

shared everything. Yes, she shared all of her secrets with me—well, she should have! I was her only sibling! And she would have, if her father had not sent me away to live with that wretched aunt! People are always sending me away—throwing me out like the trash! Well, she may have refused to confide in me like any normal, loving sister, but I found out. I discovered her little secrets and Hiram's, as well."

Livia cringed beneath the gag.

"Did you know that Delilah was quite prolific—that she found some strange pleasure in recording her secrets in a diary rather than discussing them with me—her only sister?" she asked with contempt. "A diary—a diary she called her best friend." She scowled.

"But, she paid for her little secrets and he will pay for his. Jack Rands? No, not quite. The prominent Mr. Hiram McDonnally with the poor, pathetic, kidnapped twin sister. I read about his secret identity."

The woman sat down in front of her.

"I could be sharing this house with you today, as Hannah, but Mr. Hiram had me sent away to live in isolation, hidden from life and the world, because I was not an adequate sister! He would not let me be his sister, either. No, again, I was not good enough! He stole my life. He stole my chance to be a sister, just like Delilah. Now, he too, shall pay." She snarled, and then laughed.

Dear Lord, what has she done to Delilah?

The woman leaned over and whispered, "You have to understand that we are dealing with a sick, very deranged man, Livia. You should thank me for sparing you the dreadful fate of becoming the wife of such a selfish monster." She stood up and raised her gaze to the ceiling above Livia. "My failure to burn down his *castle* has forced me to take further action. Stupid rain," she muttered.

Livia's thoughts turned to the fire in the east wing. *We all thought it was a lightning strike.*

Her captor's angry countenance transformed to an almost pleasant expression. Staring into space, she spoke calmly and sweetly, "All of this could have been prevented. I should be sitting in the parlor, entertaining guests, wearing expensive gowns, and jewelry. I could have been the loving aunt to Hiram's children." She snapped back with disgust, "But he spoiled it! He refused to give me any more money. I promised that I would keep his identity a secret and abandon those dreams, but, no, that was not enough. He had to send me away—but not far enough to silence me! I am right here in his birthplace," she said proudly.

We are still in the village, Livia thought.

Hiram tossed and turned in his bed. He left it to sit in the chair beneath the window, as his natural instinct to pace was lost to his weakened state.

God, I know that this is my doing, but I knew of no other humane method to deter that woman. That decision had brought pain to everyone. He lowered his head to rest in his hands.

"Please forgive me. Please protect Livy—not for me, but for her. She has so very much goodness to offer the world—so very much."

Down the hall, in Sophia's former room, Rahzvon finally fell asleep with his arms tight around Sophia. She lay staring at the ceiling and whispered, "Livia, wherever you are, do not fret.

God brought you back to my uncle; he would never take you from him."

The next day, the friends and neighbors returned to McDonnally Manor to organize a second search to comb the village and surrounding area. The tiring task was the only inducement for sleep for the village residents. In the short period that Livia had joined their community, they had come to love and respect her. She had founded the school for the younger children and had introduced a contagious contentment. Now, they shared the panic and desperation to recover her. Their efforts were great, despite being few in number with many absent by their war duties. The older children tended to the livestock and younger children, while the older members participated in the hunt. Edward took charge, as Hiram, having slept little the previous night, was operating on instinct alone.

Edward addressed the group from the front steps, "You all have your assigned duties. Go out to the moors and the woods. Check the deserted bothies, and inside every wagon and carriage. Report back here to Rahzvon with any findings. Now, be safe and make haste; a storm is brewing."

They dispersed quickly. Edward joined Hiram who was tightening the cinch on Hunter's saddle. He put a hand on Hiram's shoulder.

"Stiff upper lip, man. Naomi assures me that Livia is well. She has a sixth sense about these things. Believe her and know that every minute should not be one lost to panic, but one closer to being reunited."

Hiram glanced up. Edward's words seem to fall on deaf ears. Hiram's eyes were black with anger and animosity for Avera and little hope for finding Livia unharmed. Edward knew that his advice was useless and left to say goodbye to Naomi.

"I love you, my magic square," he said softly. "He has been pushed past his limit. I am staying with him. God only knows what he will do if he finds Avera."

"Be careful, love. God's speed."

"Say a prayer for all of us."

Naomi nodded. They shared a quick farewell kiss and Edward mounted up.

The ill weather grew worse, as did Hiram's temperament. At nightfall, he blasted through the front door. "Rahzvon!"

"In here!" Rahzvon called from the study.

"Well?" he shouted.

Rahzvon shook his head. Hiram was breathing hard; wearing a crazed expression of fear and anger. Hiram turned to the hall, looking in both directions. He ran upstairs to Livia's room, searching—still searching. He shot back out to the corridor and then his pace slowed as he moved to his bedchamber.

In less than a minute, the furnishings surrounding Hiram's large four-poster bed were reduced to rubble. Rahzvon stood at the bottom of the staircase with closed eyes. The sounds of crashing and Hiram's cries would be forever ingrained in his memory. Empathetic, Rahzvon knew that he would have done the same, if it were Sophia missing.

He slowly returned to the study and sat down at Hiram's desk with Guillaume's maps, returned with no results, spread before him. Weeping in the hall drew him to Hannah who was sitting on the bottom step.

"Rahzvon, we have to find her," she sobbed.

"We shall." He gently patted her back with his bandaged hands.

Shortly thereafter, family members attempted to speak with Hiram, who was locked in his room. His words of dismissal left them all feeling frustrated and helpless. They retired to face another day of searching, but where, they did not know.

Hiram, drenched in sweat, with his shredded shirt before him, sat on the floor surrounded by porcelain shards, shattered boards and torn fabric. It was quiet. The moonlight shone on the tiny brass toad in his palm. He looked at it curiously.

"Where is she? We cannot live without her." He closed his fist around the cold metal. "I need her," he mumbled and lowered his head.

Ominous clouds moved across the summer moon. The dark loneliness closed in around him. The grandfather clock tolled hour after hour. Sleep did not come for the Master of McDonnally Manor. At the striking of two in the silent hours of the morning, Hiram, with an overpowering urge to revisit the west wing, pulled his ripped jacket from the bed and found his way through the trashed items to the door.

He lifted the oil lamp, burning on the hall table, and carried it downstairs. He paused at every room in hopes of seeing Livia's face and then continued on to the west wing.

He opened the door to the school's large common room when he noticed a dim light in the kitchen. He quickly doused the lamp and silently watched the shadows dancing on the walls of the adjoining room. His heart sped. His hand slid into his pocket where his fingers tightened around the little toad. He slipped inside the doorway, placed the lamp on the floor, and moved close to the wall. Stealthily, he edged around the perimeter of the room toward the tiny kitchen. A clattering of dishware broke the silence.

Chapter IV

"Thud!"

"My life is like a broken bowl,
A broken bowl that cannot hold
One drop of water for my soul
Or cordial in the searching cold,"

—Christina Georgina Rossetti

Random thoughts penetrated Hiram's brain. Could Avera be here in the daycare kitchen? With Livy? There was no trace of them in the village. No carriage left the estate. Had they checked the entire house? Hiram squinted with confusion. He could not make sense of it. His lack of sleep hampered his rationale. He wanted to charge the kitchen, but he was afraid that he would put Livia at risk. They were in the kitchen and needed food—food for Livia? She was alive...or was she? Could it be a trap?

Believing that the end to the search may be only seconds away, his tired muscles gained new strength. The clattering stopped. Hiram listened keenly—his back pressed against the wall. There was the sound of chopping. *Is Livy in there? Is Avera with her?* His hands were sweating, now. He had to be careful, so very careful. One wrong move and it could be fatal for Livia.

He moved closer to the jamb, and then peeked inside for a split second. The vision was not as he imagined. Avera and Livia were not present. It was a large gruff-looking man. Who was he and how did he get in? The grounds were guarded.

Hiram knew that apprehending the man was not an option; matching his size was not sufficient. Hiram's strength was depleted and the intruder was using a knife to prepare his meal. Hiram controlled his breathing and risked one more glimpse. The stranger was moving back away toward the wine cellar. Hiram watched as the silhouette faded to the point of total darkness.

Dear God, you brought me here—she's in the cellar! Livy, I want to help you.. I have to think. He ran his hand across his beard several times then back through his hair.

She was down there—probably bound and gagged. Avera and that savage were with her. There could be more. Avera was determined to punish him. She may have no regard for her own life and may sacrifice it if necessary. The man could take him down in an instant. They probably had weapons, but he could get assistance, but— not the servants. There was no time to get the sheriff. Rahzvon's hands were damaged; Albert was too old. Guillaume was definitely not an option. Edward? No, he could never risk losing him, as well. He could not think clearly. What chance would he have alone?

He imagined traversing the stairwell to the cellar, and meeting up with Avera's armed assistant. He had to do something quickly, before it was too late. He prayed it would not be. He thought for a few more seconds when it hit him— the main kitchen entrance to the cellar!

He pulled off his boots and walked back to the hall as light-footed as possible to return to the kitchen in the main part of the house. Once in the corridor, he sat down on the bench, replaced his boots, and moved swiftly to the kitchen. He scowled at the sight of it being lighted, and guardedly peered inside. He fell back to the wall, rolled his eyes upward, and let out a frustrated sigh. He entered.

"Zigmann, what—?"

Shocked by the unexpected voice, Guillaume jumped with a start, nearly dropping his scone to the floor. "Mr. McDonnally!" he said, catching his breath and the scone. "I hope you have no objection. We have no, well, scones at the cottage...care to join me? God knows that you need to keep up your strength."

Hiram said nothing, focused on the door to the pantry leading to the wine cellar.

"Sir, perhaps, you should retire. It is very late. Not to worry, we shall find Miss Nichols. I know it—it is just a matter of time. She must still be here in Lochmoor Glen, although we—"

Hiram tightened his lips, and then whispered, "Zigmann she *is* here!"

"Of course, she is, and we shall bring her—"

"Blasted, Zigmann! She is here—right here!" he said through clenched teeth.

Guillaume cocked his head, "Do you mean that she has returned?"

Hiram tightened his fists, "Nay, man, she is here! In the cellar!"

Guillaume shook his head and half-smiled. "Now, Mr. McDonnally, I think that you need to go back upstairs and—"

Hiram grabbed Guillaume by the shoulders and shook him as he spoke. "God help me, but I need you Guillaume!"

Guillaume swallowed and shrunk away, uncomfortably from his grasp. "Now, sir, I know that you miss her; she is your life. I feel the same way about Allison. But sometimes when we experience a terrible shock we tend to be confused and—"

Hiram moved into his face and continued in a frustrated whisper, "Do you not understand English? She is in the cellar...at least I think that she is."

Guillaume gave him a sympathetic half-hearted smile.

"Do not look at me as though I am not of sound mind. I tell you that I went to the west wing! There was a man in the kitchen!"

Guillaume grimaced at the tale, truly believing that Hiram's mind was gone.

Hiram grabbed Guillaume by the shirtfront. "Zigmann, he took food to the cellar!"

Guillaume stared fearfully into Hiram's dark, raging gaze. "I believe you. You may release me."

Hiram released his grip. "I have had little sleep. I need a plan. I think Avera has her in the cellar. Are you not a cartographer or something?" he asked with desperation.

"An architect, actually. So you *really* believe that Avera may be below us, with Miss Nichols?"

Hiram glared at him.

"Mr. McDonnally, we should get help!"

"Shh! Nay, sit down."

He sat down across from Hiram.

"There is a large accomplice, as well. If we storm the cellar, it could be fatal for Livy. They may have weapons and their food supply is the school kitchen."

"We can cut it off—barricade the door to it."

"Or remove the food," Hiram said, selecting an apple from the bowl on the table. "Nay, Livy may need the food. This is absurd; we have to get her out of there."

"Sir, we need to get the constable."

"Nay, it is too risky for Livy, if she is still—" Hiram lowered his head.

"Sir, look at me. Avera would not stay here if Livia were not alive. She would leave a note and go."

"She did leave a note...on the chalkboard."

"Yes, but why would they stay here and be taking food to the cellar?"

Hiram crushed the apple in his palm. "The man may have no connection; he may be a vagabond, held up in my wine cellar. We have to find out, Zigmann."

Guillaume left the chair, taking a bite of his scone.

"Where are you going?" Hiram demanded.

"To fetch Rahzvon."

"Nay! I do not want Sophia endangered."

"Very well, then, we shall have to take this entrance and investigate," Guillaume said bravely. "We have to be very careful." He broke away half of his scone and handed it to Hiram. "Here, eat this; you will need the energy."

Hiram looked at the piece blankly while Guillaume removed the flashlight from the drawer. Hiram shoved the scone into his mouth, opened the drawer in the sideboard, and removed the butcher's knife.

They opened the door in the pantry, and yes, the steep cellar steps were creaky. Hiram prayed that Livia and her captors were in the section of the cellar beneath the school and not in the original room beneath the main house, that he and Guillaume would enter. When Hiram, determined to stay on the wagon, had first returned to live at the estate, he had all of the wine removed from beneath the kitchen and moved to the far end—out of temptation's reach.

Led by the little beam of light, Hiram and Guillaume found the first cellar room void of life, with the exception of a family of field mice. The two men continued slowly through the passage.

Several minutes later, the door to the wine cellar room loomed before them. They paused, exchanged an apprehensive look and moved closer to the door. They could hear voices beyond. Guillaume glanced at Hiram, who nodded. They moved closer, straining to decipher the conversation. Two voices were discernible, but their muffled words were beyond recognition. Guillaume noted a crack in the slat near the bottom of the door. He lowered down to the dirt for a view of the inhabitants.

"Ah!" Guillaume stood up.

"What?" Hiram whispered.

"They are drinking your wine!" Guillaume whispered in his ear.

Hiram gave Zigmann a frustrated nudge to return to the ground.

Guillaume tugged gently on Hiram's trouser cuff, to join him. Hiram peered through the slat at the woman. Her hair was mousy brown. *Is that Avera?* He remembered her with jet-black hair like his own. *Of course, she darkened it, to convince me that she was Hannah.* There was the man—the man who was in the school kitchen. But where was Livia? His heart sped. She was not there. *Then why are they here? What have they done with her? he panicked.*

Sophia tossed and turned, waking every few minutes in worry over Livia's well-being. She lit the lamp and began reading *The Invisible Man.* Her lack of concentration, led her to abandon it. She dimmed the flame, slipped on her robe, and entered the hall. To her surprise, the lamp that sat on the hall table was missing. She returned to her room to retrieve the lamp from their bedside, and tiptoed back to the hall. She moved gingerly toward the stairs, which led to the third floor bedroom, once belonging to her grandmother. Sophia, like Hiram, found the room to serve as a chapel of sorts—a sanctuary in time of need or private meditation.

She turned the silver key with the green tassel that hung from the keyhole and entered. After turning up the lamp, she found the familiar surroundings to be neither eerie, nor uninviting. The room offered a sense of comforting warmth and security. She looked up at the portrait of her grandmother Amanda, Hannah and Hiram's mother. She took a place at the dressing table and examined the silver hairbrush, comb and hand mirror—gifts from her grandfather Geoffrey. Another glimpse at the portrait, then at her reflection confirmed their likely, but extraordinary resemblance.

"Grandmother, we are in a terrible state down here. Livia is missing...but I suppose that you are well aware of that. Uncle Hiram—all of us are out of our minds with worry. Oh, I did not tell you! I am—Rahzvon, that is my wonderful husband—he burnt his hands saving me—we are having a baby—a *bairn*, as you would say. Did you know that Rahzvon and I were destined to be together? Yes, it was a miracle; my mother delivered me on blankets from Kosdrev in the shipping office in Par—"

THUD!

Sophia stopped short at the sound above her. She slowly looked upward. "Grandmother?" she whispered anxiously.

Then a second *thud*, not as loud as the first.

Sophia's eyes widened. She sat motionless, staring fearfully upward to the ceiling that shared the floor of the attic storeroom. She listened intensely. *That was not Grandmother and too loud to be a bat or a rat.* She held her hand to her heart, trying to remain calm.

THUD!

Sophia grabbed the lamp and flew from the bench into the hall, down the stairs to the second floor. Without taking time to breath, she ran to her bedroom and jumped onto the bed.

"Wake up! Rahzvon, wake up!" she yelled, shaking him violently.

"Uh!" He woke with a start. "What is it?"

"There is something in the attic!"

He squinted against the light. "That is why you woke me?" He dropped to the pillow and closed his eyes. "Go back to sleep," he mumbled.

"Rahzvon Sierzik, I demand that you listen to me! This is serious! It is alive!"

Rahzvon's eyelids slowly opened, "It is that book you have been reading, your imagination—"

"Rahzvon Sierzik, I tell you there is something in the attic! It may be a prowler!"

"At his hour? It is probably a servant," he said groggily.

"A servant? At three o'clock in the morning?"

"Phia, go to sleep, I will check in the morning."

"Go to sleep? How am I to sleep with Livia missing and people in the attic?" she scorned.

Rahzvon lay still. His eyes flew open. He sat up and grabbed Sophia. "Did you say that there were people in the attic? Did you hear voices?" he demanded.

"No, a dropping sound. Only louder, like someone dropped something—but three times!"

"Where, Phia? Where?"

"I was in Grandmother's room, talking to her, when I heard it in the storeroom above me, in the attic."

Rahzvon slid from the bed. "Blast these

bandages! Phia, help me with my trousers and boots!"

Sophia pulled up his trousers, buttoned them and then held each boot. "You know, soon I will look like Humpty Dumpty helping you."

Rahzvon did not hear a word; his thoughts were focused on the attic. He was in near panic.

"Rahzvon? What are you thinking?"

"If it is an intruder, Hiram needs to know. Come along."

They rushed to Hiram's bedroom and knocked twice without response. They opened the door and held up the lantern that lighted the disaster.

Sophia's jaw dropped, "Great Scott, he has done it again."

"It is no wonder. Well, he is not here," Rahzvon said, closing the door.

"Do you think that he is in the storeroom?"

"We need to check Livia's room. Wait here." Rahzvon left Sophia standing in the dark, took the lamp and ran down the hall. "Not there, either. I am going downstairs. I will be back in a minute." He checked the rooms for a light in the study, parlor, dining room, and kitchen. He returned to Sophia. "He is not down there. He must be out looking for Livia or maybe *he* is in the attic."

"Should we waken Mother?"

"No, let her sleep. Follow me."

"I can carry the lamp now, I know that it hurts your hands," Sophia offered, taking it from him."

"Thank you."

"Are we going up to the attic?"

"*We* are not. I am."

"Rahzvon, I am afraid," she confessed, as they approached the door to the attic stairwell.

"Open the door, as quietly as possible and remain here."

"But you have no way of defending yourself," she said nervously. "Your hands—I need to go with you."

"First of all, it is probably Hiram and secondly, if it is not, I am not going to depend on the expectant mother of my child to defend me. I am going to investigate, that is all." He lowered the flame on the lamp before opening the door. "Now, wait here. Do not follow me. Phia, if, perchance, I call out...fetch your mother and get help. Promise you will hold the stair rail."

"I promise. Oh darling, kiss me first."

He leaned down, kissed her and then stepped lightly towards the attic rooms.

"Be careful. *Bosiw ed guth,*" she whispered, as he vanished from the steps.

Rahzvon began his journey to the storeroom. The gabled windows offered enough celestial light to allow his careful passage. It would soon be daylight.

Upon reaching the door to the storeroom, he placed his ear against it. Nothing. He squatted down and looked through the keyhole. His heart raced at the sight. Rahzvon could not believe his eyes; Livia was lying bound and gagged on the floor. No one else appeared to be with her. He waited a minute more, wondering if there was someone on the wall near the door. He tried to manipulate the doorknob. It seemed to be locked. He took the chance and whispered, "Livia, Livia, it is me, Rahzvon."

When she did not respond, a cold shudder ran through him. Without a second thought, he rammed his right shoulder into the door, but it did not budge. He raised his bandaged hands to his mouth and began tearing away the gauze with his teeth. He turned to the broken chair laying on the floor next to him and heaved it into the door with one very loud "AGH!" as the pain shot from his hands up through his forearms to his shoulders.

Hearing his cry, Sophia ran down the hall screaming, taking care to hold the stair railing. "Help! Help! Mother!"

Hannah met her in the hall. "Sophia, what has happened?"

Sophia was out of breath and frantic. "They got him! My husband!"

"Who Sophia?"

"The people in the attic!"

Chapter V

"Timing"

"What fortitude the soul contains
That it can so endure
The accent of a coming foot
The opening of a door!"

—Emily Dickinson

"People in the attic?" Hannah said with horror. "We have to get Hiram!"

"Mama, he is gone!"

"Then Albert. Go to the servant quarters and get Miles and Roy. I will grab my robe and go for Albert."

The two panicked women were back in minutes, accompanied by the servants, caretaker, and Eloise. They rushed toward the steps leading to the attic, when a figure appeared at the end of the corridor.

"Rahzvon?" Sophia ran to him. In his arms was the limp body of Livia Nichols with hands and feet bound. "Livia! Is she—?"

"No," Rahzvon reassured. "But I think she is ill from lack of nourishment."

Sophia gasped at the blood covering Livia's dress.

"Not to worry, Little One, it is mine."

"Yours?" She could not breathe as her eyes fell upon his torn and bleeding hands.

Rahzvon turned to Roy. "Rusty is up there, bound, as well. He has fared better than Livia, but he is desperate to be rescued."

Roy hesitated. "Miles, you go. He is more familiar with you." Miles nodded at Roy and ran to the attic.

With tear-filled eyes, Hannah choked out the instructions for Roy to carry Livia to her room. "Eloise, I know that you are concerned about Rusty, but you must wrap Rahzvon's hands."

"At once, Mum, I shall fetch towels, bandaging, and broth for Miss Nichols."

"Albert, please, have Dr. Lambert summoned immediately," Hannah asked.

He nodded and left.

***

Meanwhile, two floors below them, Guillaume presented his plan to Hiram to apprehend Avera and her assistant in the wine cellar of the west wing.

"I will go back upstairs to the kitchen, then to the west wing and divert their attention at the entrance to the school kitchen. When you see them respond, you make loud noises here at this end. The man has no firearm that I can see. If he does, it is in his jacket several feet away. Besides, they have been drinking, so their reaction time will be hampered. I will then sneak up from behind and jump him when you present yourself in the doorway with the knife. How does that sound?" Guillaume whispered.

Hiram squinted, trying to process the sequence. His brain was not up to speed, but his desperation to find Livia, led him to agree without hesitation.

Guillaume disappeared to carry out the first part of the plan. He entered the kitchen from the pantry door of the cellar.

"Guillaume!" his mother reprimanded. "Where have you been?"

"I—"

"I do not have time for your excuses! Quick rush these towels up to Hannah. It is an emergency!"

"What?"

"Go son, hurry, Sophia will explain."

"Sophia—is she?"

"Get going, son!"

Guillaume panicked and ran with the load of towels to the second floor and frantically into Sophia's room. "Sophia, is it time?" he asked, out of breath.

"Time for what?" she replied, confused.

"Time for the baby, of course!"

"No, that shan't happen for many months. Here, I need those for his hands."

Guillaume looked at Rahzvon's hands in horror. "Good grief! What happened?"

"It is nothing, Zigmann."

"Nothing, it looks as though you fought off a rabid dog."

"I am fine."

Sophia gently blotted his mangled hands to prepare them for Eloise to bandage.

"Agh!" Rahzvon groaned. "Zigmann, go help Hannah. See if she needs anything."

"Hannah? Do not tell me that you had a brawl with your mother-in-law!"

Sophia looked at Guillaume with disappointment. "Guillaume Zigmann, you are incorrigible. Go help Mother. She is in Livia's room."

Thoroughly perplexed, Guillaume wandered into the hall where he met his mother.

"Son, take this broth to Hannah. Dr. Lambert will be arriving soon and I need to bandage Rahzvon's wounds."

Guillaume passed Miles carrying Rusty, who was now free from his bindings and anxious to get down. Miles placed the wriggling dachshund to the floor.

"How's my boy?" Guillaume reached down to pet him.

Rusty, thrilled to see his family member, hopped around on his dwarfed legs and followed Guillaume down the hall.

Down in the wine cellar, Hiram waited and

watched at the crack in the door, thinking, *it shan't be long, now, before they will turn to Guillaume's distraction.*

During all the commotion, Naomi's visiting cat, Patience, ventured into the west wing—a place of interest during her previous residence with Naomi at the manor. Delighted to discover the articles strewn about the floor of the school storeroom, the cat crept about them curiously, sniffing one article after another. The aroma of fresh cut meat lured her to the kitchenette. She sat up on her haunches, sniffing the air before leaping to the table to lick the soiled cutting board. After a brief paw washing, she approached the door to the cellar, which was usually cracked open so that she could perform her duties as top mouser. As the door was closed, the distraught cat planted its front paws on the door and began scratching and mewing with disapproval.

For Hiram, the moment he had been anticipating had arrived. Avera and the man turned toward the steps, signaling Hiram to make the surprise attack. He jumped to his feet and blasted through the door presenting his kitchen weapon.

As to be expected, Avera and her accomplice turned toward Hiram with alarm.

"Do not move!" Hiram demanded. They froze, as instructed while Hiram looked beyond them, waiting for Guillaume's attack.

However, Guillaume was standing with the hot broth on the second floor. Hannah motioned for him to follow. "Bring it quickly, before it cools."

Upon seeing Livia tucked beneath the covers, Guillaume nearly dropped the tureen. "Livia?"

"Shh!" Hannah reprimanded.

"She is back! Hiram shall be so—" His mouth opened wide. "Oh no! Hiram!"

Frantic, Guillaume tore from the room. He returned only to leave the tureen, before sprinting full-speed down the staircase and through the corridor to the west wing. Rusty chased him, barking wildly. Guillaume stopped midway.

"Go back, Rusty!" he said sternly, pointing down the hall.

Rusty took his upright begging position, balanced on his haunches and continued barking.

"No, Rusty, NO! Go back!"

The pup refused and followed. Guillaume stopped, bent down and scooped him up. "You are impossible!"

Guillaume ran back to the main kitchen. When he entered, his eyes nearly left their sockets. Avera and her accomplice were tied to the kitchen chairs with Hiram standing over them.

"Playing with your dog, Zigmann?" Hiram asked scornfully.

"Yes, sir, I mean no, sir," Guillaume stammered, trying to hold onto his growling, enraged dog—ready to attack the flinching captives.

"Get him out of here," Hiram instructed. However, in seeing the sense of relief in his captives, he reconsidered. "On second thought, stay Zigmann. Now," Hiram turned to Avera, "Where is Livy? What have you done with her?"

Avera said nothing.

"But, sir—" Guillaume interrupted.

"Put him down, Guillaume."

"With all due respect, sir, Livia—"

Hiram's tired, dark eyes flashed angrily. "Put

the blasted dog down, now!

"But, sir, he will tear them to bits!"

"I should have done in him, when I had the chance," Avera muttered.

"Now, Zigmann!"

Avera let out a scream. "No! No! She is in the attic!"

Hiram's face lightened with new hope. "Watch them!" In his flight up the backstairs to the east wing, he ignored Guillaume's calls to deter him.

Hiram, taking three steps at a time mounted the attic stairs, shouting, "Livy! Livy!" He passed through the vacant storeroom to the opposite end, calling, "Livy, where are you!" He upturned grayed wicker baskets, threw open lids of four trunks and tossed aside crate after crate as he stepped past the splintered door. *What's happened here?* Ringing wet with sweat, his panic turned to rage. He bolted back to the kitchen.

A minute later, he was on them, hands at their throats, he bellowed, "Where is she?"

"Hiram! Stop it!" Hannah demanded. Rusty instantly stopped barking. "Hiram we have found Livia. She is well. She is in her room."

Hiram's heavy breathing slowed. He squinted with confusion. "Livy, in her room?" he mumbled.

Guillaume stepped back cautiously, "I tried to tell you."

Hannah gently coaxed, "Come away from them, Hiram, and see for yourself."

With one last threatening glimpse, Hiram released his grip. Hannah took his arm.

His pace quickened as he entered the staircase. He could not believe it—it was over. He was going to see her, to hold her. His life could begin again.

Hannah poked her head through the doorway of Livia's room. "Please, give them some privacy."

Eloise and an assisting maid quickly exited, as Hiram entered. Hannah closed the door behind him. She sobbed in the hall, as she listened to her brother cry for the first time.

After Dr. Lambert's visit, Hiram lay down on the bed next to Livia and placed his arm over her. They slept several hours. Hiram awoke to the soft touch of Livia's finger tracing his black brows.

"Hello, my love," she whispered.

"Ah, my sweet Livy, what have I done to you?" he said with remorse.

"Don't blame yourself. She is a very ill woman." She ran her hand down his cheek. "Let us forget about her and begin again. "Good morning."

"Good morning, or is it afternoon?"

"It does not matter to me. I could stay here forever. This is the longest duration that I have spent with you in weeks," she said, smiling.

"Aye, and to think that we slept through the greater part of it. From this day forward, I shall treasure every moment with you and not a single harsh word shall cross my lips."

Livia grinned skeptically, but was pleased with the promise, however unlikely it seemed.

The McDonnally money expedited Avera's trial at which she and her accomplice were convicted. Hiram kept his promise to remain calm and collected, even at the trial, until one rare Sunday mid-morning.

"This is for you, Miss Nichols." Roy delivered a package to Livia, while she and Hiram dined in the garden.

"Thank you, Roy. Do you mind if I open it?" Livia asked Hiram.

"Of course not. I am as curious as you are."

"Roy, please wait and take these wrappings," Livia instructed, opened the box, and unwrapped the item, within. "Oh! Another one from Russia!" She lifted out the nesting doll. "He is an angel for remembering."

"Who? Who is an angel?" Hiram tried to retain his smile.

"Look, it is exquisite. Is it not beautiful, Roy?"

"Quite a piece of folk art, Miss Nichols." He gathered up the wrapping.

She grinned ear-to-ear. "Yes, it is perfect. I cannot believe that he located me. You may go now, Roy."

"Yes, Ma'am."

"Who? Who located you?" Hiram asked impatiently, no longer smiling.

"Benjamin, of course. Just watch this, Hiram." She opened the doll and began disassembling them and lining them up on the table. "Look—eight of them. Are they not absolutely adorable?" Hiram was silent.

"Roy agreed," Livia said, admiring them.

Hiram still did not answer her question, but had a few of his own. "Who is Benjamin and why did he send this?"

"An acquaintance. He sends me a new Matryoshka doll each time he tours Russia. With the war, though, it will probably be the last for awhile."

"I have not seen these."

"Why Hiram, they have been around for years. The first was created in 1890, I believe...at the

Children's Education Workshop. That is what Benjamin told me."

"That is not what I meant, I—"

She held up the smallest. "Is it not adorable? They are named for the Russian word for mother, *matry*. Benjamin saw the largest with forty-eight pieces in St. Petersburg last year!"

"That is all very fine, but where are the others? I can assume that you gave them to charity."

"No, no. They are safe at the home of Benjamin's nana. I was traveling and did not want to take all of them with me."

"Good grief! How many are there?"

"Sets or individual dolls?"

"*Livy!*"

"Dozens, I suspect. He traveled extensively. I can send for them, now that I am settled."

Hiram sat back, scowling.

"I love them," Livia sighed. "Look at their lovely peasant costumes."

"Livy, I cannot have strange men sending you gifts while you are married to me."

"Am I hearing a harsh word? Besides, Benjamin is not a stranger, and you and I are not yet married," she said calmly, opening the dolls and restacking them.

"I am simply stating the necessity and sanctity of male territorial rights. Livy, are you condoning this arrogant man's behavior?"

"His kind, generous nature?"

"His blatant bribery."

"Bribery?" Livia mumbled and read the note inside the box.

"It is apparent that he sends these with the intention of retaining a relationship with you, and what is worse—you delight in it. What does the note say?"

Livia placed the top half on the largest doll and looked up at him with disappointment. Hiram had never spoken to her with such degree of disapproval. She felt his words to be hurtful, but not solely without merit. However, her rights as a single woman were threatened. "I apologize. I was not aware that my receiving mail invaded your personal territory. When he delivers the others, I shall take care to store them elsewhere. Perhaps Naomi would not mind, if I display them at Brachney Hall."

"When he delivers them?" His black eyes grew intense.

"I am not entitled to visitors, either?" she asked innocently.

Hiram threw down his napkin and left through the garden gate.

Sophia, too, was in definite need of an attitude adjustment. While wiping the wounds on Rahzvon's hands in preparation for the new bandages, she voiced her disapproval.

"You had to be the hero. You never gave one thought to your hands. Now, I will be bandaging them for eternity. And do you care to explain as to why you felt that your wife was not worthy of your little secret about Avera's letter? That letter was under *my* table! Not Livia's," she scorned, pulling the gauze tighter.

"Ow! Be careful."

Sophia released his hand and looked away.

"Phia, please look at me, I wanted to tell you; you know that I do not approve of secrets."

She turned back and retorted, "I know no

such thing."

"It was solely for your protection. I did not want to worry you with an unfounded accusation about your Uncle or one of your kin."

"You did not mind worrying Livia about Uncle Hiram!"

"Do not bring Livia into this discussion. The poor woman has suffered enough."

"And I have not? Are these not my husband's hands which shall not caress my face for another fortnight, because he *had* to rescue her?"

"I cannot believe that you are jealous of Livia. She nearly lost her life at the hand of that lunatic."

"Poor, poor Livia—does she occupy your every thought?" Sophia shouted, dropping the roll of bandages and running from the room.

"Phia!"

Crying, she ran into her mother's arms.

"What goes on here, Sophia?" Hannah asked, embracing her daughter.

"Nothing, absolutely nothing. All he thinks about is her!" She pulled away and left for the backdoor.

Entering the garden, Sophia saw her adversary, Livia, seated at the table, but she continued on, through the garden gate to the barn. To her surprise, she found her uncle sitting on a bale of hay. Out of breath and sniffling, she stood before him without words to address him. Hiram left the bale and put a comforting arm around her.

"Sophia, what has happened? You should not be running and getting upset in your condition."

"At least, *you* have some concern for my well-being."

"Am I to assume your unhappy state is a product of Mr. Sierzik's behavior? You know that he was quite the selfless hero, again."

"Selfless, perhaps, but with little regard for his wife and unborn child!" She marched over to Duff, who stirred uneasily in his stall with her arrival. "Should he not be out running free?"

"Nay, he is lame in his right front leg. Now, would you care to explain your derogatory comment about your husband?"

"No. I guess it does not concern you that my husband is infatuated with your, your—"

"My horse?"

"*No*! Livia! Uncle Hiram, open your eyes! Do you not see that my swooning husband would do anything—risk anything for her? In fact—he did! Do you need more proof?" She began to sob, "Uncle Hiram, we are losing them—to each other."

He drew her into his chest and comforted her. "Sophia, I am not quite certain that I ever had Livy. There may be someone else...someone who has touched her heart in a manner in which I have failed."

"I knew it," she wept.

"Not Rahzvon. He loves you. A man can recognize it in another man's eyes. He looks at you...well, you are his life. Nay, he adores Livy, but I fear another man, like ill-weather, is unexpected, but guaranteed to return."

Sophia looked up with sad eyes, "Who? What man?"

"You need not fret over it, nor worry about Rahzvon having designs on Livy. He may be bold, but he loves life entirely too much, to tread that path. Go now, and make amends. I need time to think."

Sophia left the barn bursting with curiosity of Livia's suitor. She was disturbed by the prospect, but grateful it was not Rahzvon.

"Sophia!" Livia called to her, as she entered the garden."Sophia redirected her steps toward her.

"How is Rahzvon?" Livia asked.

"His hands are badly damaged, but they shall heal *again*. I am seeing to that."

"Sophia, I am very grateful to Rahzvon, but sorry that the two of you have suffered for it. I know that you were looking forward to his hands finally being healed and now that has been delayed."

"That is a very thoughtful apology." Sophia sat down next to her. "Who is this man who cannot hold a candle to my uncle? Is this from him?" Sophia picked up the nesting dolls.

"*Sophia,* why would you ask such a question?"

"A simple inquiry. Who is he?"

"These are from a friend."

"Was he always *only* a friend?"

Livia lowered her head. When she looked up there were more than Sophia's pair of questioning eyes upon her. Hiram, too, waited for her response. Livia nervously fled to her room.

Several minutes later, Hiram entered her room. She was packing a bag. "What is the meaning of this?" he demanded.

"Your jealousy is ridiculous. If our relationship is to survive until our marriage, I cannot remain here. I am taking a room at the inn." Livia closed her trunk and latched it. "I love you, Hiram, I would like to continue with my school, if you find it permissible."

Hiram snatched her pocketbook from the bed and stuffed it under his arm.

Chapter VI

"Benjamin"

"Throw away thy rod
Throw away thy wrath;
Oh my God,
Take the gentle path."

—George Herbert

"Hiram, give me my pocketbook, please. This is for your own good," Livia said calmly.

"Livy, do not talk to me as though I were a child."

"Then, do not behave as one. Please, give it to me."

"Come and get it."

"I shan't play games with you."

"Aye? Games seem to be your expertise."

"What are you implying, Mr. McDonnally?"

"You know me better than anyone and yet you are intent on torturing me with your past. It is a hobby with you."

"Ah! I torment you with *my* past? How dare you? How is it that I was bound, starved, and gagged in your attic? Was your *past* not responsible?"

"That was low, Livy. I take offense. I did not invite Avera here to torture you."

"And I did not ask Benjamin to send me the doll sets."

"Why do you keep them?"

"They are beautiful pieces of art and I love them for just that reason. Now, if you would, please, give me my pocketbook."

"Give me the dolls and I shall."

Livia's eyes widened. She popped open the trunk and removed the dolls. "Very well! Here!"

Hiram hesitated, feeling embarrassed for his juvenile behavior and tossed her purse and the dolls on the bed, and left.

Livia arrived at the inn, only to find it without vacant rooms. Finding this first in Lochmoor Glen, she was highly suspicious and certain that her angry counterpart had arranged the inconvenience. With no other choice, she did the unthinkable and let the room on the floor above the pub—a room normally occupied by inebriated regulars, unfit to return to their homes.

Hiram went about his duties, trying to ignore the loneliness and misery of Livia's absence. He had barely recovered from the incident of her kidnapping, before she was gone again. However, his ego did not allow him to plead for her return. He curbed his frustration through hours of hard work on the farms by day and paperwork by night. He avoided her for fear of giving in, surrendering to her hold on him.

On the third day of their estrangement, Livia's miniature stove, pots, and pans for the classroom were delivered. Livia, equally discontent with the solitude, utilized the delivery as a means to speak with Hiram—to thank him for his generosity.

"Eloise, I am about to leave. Has Mr. McDonnally returned to take supper?"

"Yes, he is in the garden. We miss you, Mum."

"I miss all of you, as well. How is Roy working out?"

"He is a hard worker and a pleasure to work with."

"Glad to hear it."

"The biscuits for Parents' Night are in the covered basket in the pantry, safe from snooping men."

Livia laughed. "Thank you. Now, I need to speak with Hiram."

"You are welcome."

Livia made her way, winding through the shrub-lined paths, past the numerous blooming flowerbeds. She finally saw Hiram's silhouette, sitting with one knee up on the wall, facing the woods. She paused, primped her hair and continued.

"Good evening, Hiram."

"Livia." He did not turn to greet her.

Livia? He is upset. "I would like, but a minute of your time."

He swung around to face her. "That is the problem. You are content with only a minute of my presence." He slipped down from the wall and walked past her toward the rear entry of the house. Livia watched in astonishment, as he disappeared. She dropped to the bench behind her.

"Livia?" a soft-spoken voice addressed her.

She wiped her eyes and mumbled, "Good evening, Rahzvon."

"Here." He pulled a handkerchief from his trouser pocket and handed it to her. "You, living above the pub? He should be ashamed. He is a foolish, stubborn man, and you cannot expect much from him with his pride. He is hurting as much as he is angry. Give him a little more time. May I?" He looked to the bench.

"Yes, please sit."

"Livia, no one knows better than I that living under the same roof with Hiram can be intolerable, at the least. It is his home, of which he is lord and master. I understand your position— living elsewhere until you are married. But at this rate, that may be a very long time. Might I offer you some advice?'

Livia nodded.

"Meet with him somewhere, anywhere but here. A neutral place. Talk to him. Rekindle the fire in your relationship. He is a man—it won't take much, I can assure you. I know from my own experience in living with Phia, that in most cases, a McDonnally will die brooding before taking the initiative to make amends. We have all noted the result of this rift. You are not happy at the school and you should be; it is your first Parents' Night. And Hiram has been a beast since you left. In fact, Albert and I have been placing bets on which one of us will receive the brunt of his discontentment, next. Guillaume has steered clear of the mansion, entirely."

"I tried to thank him for the children's kitchen set, but he did not give me the opportunity."

"Not here, in his territory. You need to speak with him where he is powerless. Not in his castle, Livia." Rahzvon looked up to Hiram's bedroom window. "Ah, we are being watched, again."

She looked up, in time to see Hiram move away from the window.

"Livia, go back to your room. I will give him the message that you want to speak with him at your room above the pub."

"At my room?"

"Yes, it is perfect; small and without escape. Smother him with kindness. Besides, he will pity you for living in such a pathetic residence." Rahzvon stood and offered her his hand. "Come along, I will get you a driver. Trust me, Livia."

Rahzvon spoke with Roy to order a carriage and then hurried up to Hiram's room and knocked.

"Who is it?"

"Rahzvon."

Hiram opened the door. "Hello."

"Good evening, sir."

"Let me take this opportunity to offer my gratitude in rescuing Livy; I am indebted to you."

"In that case, might you do me a favor?"

"What might that be?"

"Go to the pub—I mean to Livia's room, over the pub. She is there and would like to speak with you."

Hiram turned away. "She asked you to deliver this message?"

"Not exactly. Hiram you know how foolish and stubborn women can be. You cannot expect much from them with their pride. She is hurting as much as she is angry. I understand your position. Go to her. Her students are suffering from her ill temper. Smother her with kindness. Her room is small with no place to escape your chivalry. Take pity on her for her inadequate housing. I am certain that if you invite her to return, she will."

Hiram ran his finger across the doorjamb. "I did have something to give her." He reached into his pocket and grasped the Swedish carved horse that he had purchased at the mercantile.

"Good. Go now," Rahzvon encouraged.

Rahzvon went directly to the room that he shared with Sophia. She was sitting on the bed finishing the last chapter of *The Invisible Man.*

"*You* seem to be the invisible man. Where have you been?"

"Phia, I can nearly guarantee that Hiram and Livia will be back in each other's arms within the hour."

"How do you know this?"

"It does not matter, Little One. Peace will soon reign again." He crawled up next to her and placed his hand on her belly. "Now, tell me everything that we shall need to purchase for this little angel. Gaelon assures me that it won't be long before we have money to spare."

Sophia's face lighted with pure pleasure. "Well, wee gowns, of course."

"How many do you think?"

"Not many. Our daughter shall not spit up her milk. She is going to be fed as God intended."

"She is?"

"Naturally."

"Oh, naturally."

Hiram's carriage stopped outside of the pub. He stepped out. The light was burning in the room above. He started for the steps leading to the second floor room. He placed his foot on the bottom step. *Smother her with kindness.* He pulled out the Dala Haus and smiled, before returning it to his pocket.

Livia saw the carriage and ran to the looking glass above the washbasin. *Very well, smother him with kindness.*

"Hiram!"

He turned to the jovial face of George Hicks. "George, what are you doing here?"

"I might ask you the very same. I have returned to examine the records of another client."

"I have an appointment with Miss Nichols," he mumbled, ashamed of her living above the pub.

"Here at the pub?"

"Nay, I was on my way to meet her."

"Aye, Livia Nichols. Did she finally confess her dealings with Thomas?" he laughed.

"Of course, she did."

"Grand. Secrets will destroy a relationship. I had a few of my own that returned to haunt me. My wife left me *and* the country *with* my two sons. Bad business, secrets. I must say that I am surprised that Thomas gave up Livia— considering what he went through."

"Went through?"

"Yes, he fought Benjamin tooth and nail for claim to her. He nearly killed the man. Well, I should let you to your engagement. Quite a prize, that young woman. Many men would give their arm to be in your shoes. Some almost have."

Benjamin? "George, I am a wee bit early, care to have a drink with me?"

"Certainly, I am in no hurry. I have no plans for the evening."

George followed Hiram into the pub. George motioned to the booth that Hiram had shared with Naomi, the day he confessed his love for Livia at Hailes Crag. He sat down feeling uneasy.

"What would be yer fancy, Mr. McDonnally?" the proprietor asked.

Hiram looked uncomfortably around the room. A scraggily man of about forty lay passed out, sprawled across a table. Two other patrons were having an arm-wrestling match at the bar, to the joy of a few cheering spectators.

"Gin for me," George announced.

Hiram glanced to the owner waiting for his order. "Nothing for now."

"Are you certain?" George asked. "I do not enjoy drinking alone."

Hiram shook his head.

The owner left and Hiram casually picked up a fork that was on the seat next to him. He tapped it on the table. "So this Benjamin was not much of a man?"

"Ah, on the contrary—a big brute, but of a gentle nature for a man his size. Yes, he cherished the very ground on which Livia walked."

Hiram held the fork up for closer observation. "And Livy—she obviously saw nothing redeeming in his character?"

"Quite the opposite—she adored him. She was stuck on him like a fly to honey cake."

Hiram jammed the fork into the tabletop.

The pub owner, who had arrived with George's gin, looked at the fork standing upright in the table. Noting Hiram's irate expression, he asked, "Is there a problem, Mr. McDonnally?"

"Aye. Excuse me, George," Hiram said, sliding from the booth. He returned to his carriage and instructed the driver to take him home.

After several minutes, Livia, curious as to why Hiram never arrived, went to the window above the street.

"It's gone," she said seeing the street vacant of Hiram's carriage. *Why would he leave?*

Disappointed, she changed into her nightgown, blew out the lantern, and climbed into bed. *Your plan failed, Rahzvon.*

Hiram rode home feeling confused and betrayed that Livia had not mentioned "Benjamin" prior to the arrival of the dolls. He tapped on the ceiling. The driver stopped the team of horses. "Driver, take me to Brachney Hall."

When he arrived at his uncle's home, he rapped impatiently at the door. The butler invited him in and directed him to the library where Edward was entering one last stamp into his album.

"Hiram, ol' man, what brings you here at this hour?" Forewarned by his nephew's deliberate stride and disgruntled expression, he asked cautiously, "Hiram, what is wrong, now?"

"Blast it, Edward! That woman has driven me to the end of my rope!"

"Miss Nettlepin, again?

Hiram's jaw tightened.

"Not Abigail?" Edward's eyes widened.

"Nay!" Hiram paced several steps across the room.

"Who is it man?" Edward asked impatiently.

"Only the so-called love of my life," he said disdainfully.

"Livia?" Edward asked Hiram.

"Edward, *that* woman. Every time I turn around, that woman has another rooster waiting at the hen house."

"Man, you have been working too long on these farms. Are you accusing Livia, that innocent creature, of encouraging her past suitors to drive you to madness?" Edward asked, grinning.

"You would not make light of this, if it was Naomi!" Hiram charged and left for his home.

Edward's smile vanished. Naomi's past with Hiram and her attachment to the earrings that Hiram had given her, flashed before him. *No it is not amusing, Hiram, but we need to put it all behind us.*

The McDonnally men were at odds with the world. Hiram returned home and went to bed without a word to anyone. The slamming of his door was warning to the servants to leave him alone. Edward was having difficulty putting the memory of the earring incident behind him.

Naomi who had returned from her walk with Heidi, her dachshund from the Dugan litter, went to check on Edward, upon hearing, "Blast it!" echoing from their library.

"A problem, dearest?" she asked, unhooking Heidi's leash.

"Hiram! Hiram and Livia. He stopped by to complain, again."

"Is that all? Well, I am exhausted. I am going up to bed. Could you unlatch my bracelet?"

Edward looked down at her wrist and attempted, but failed.

"Dear you are not at the latch."

"Why do they make these so ridiculously small and who gave you this?"

"You did. Never mind, I will ask the maid."

"We need better lighting," he grumbled raising and lowering the magnifying lens, trying to discern the markings on a stamp.

"Dear it is not the lamp; it is your failing eyesight. You need spectacles."

Edward stood up, slamming the glass onto the table. "I do not! Please, do not mention it again!"

"Very well, if you want to tote that lens around with you; you shall need it *every* time you pick up a printed page."

"The McDonnallys do not where spectacles! We do not need them!"

"Then get a monocle."

"This discussion is over, I am retiring."

Naomi let out a sigh and followed him upstairs. "Men are often thought to appear more intelligent when donning eyeglasses."

Edward stopped on the steps. "Not another

word."

"Very well, walk through life with vague images of the beauty surrounding you. I do not mind if you have no interest in detail."

Edward tightened his fists and entered the bedroom.

"I am inviting Livia and Hiram to share dinner with us, tomorrow," she said, sitting down at her dressing table.

"Why?"

"Because Livia's Parents' Night is Thursday evening."

"I am inquiring as to why you feel the need to be the peacemaker for Hiram and his women?" Edward snapped.

"Mr. McDonnally, you need not be short with me because you are frustrated with your vision," she said, managing to unlatch her bracelet. She laid it out carefully on the table and glanced back at Edward, sitting on the bed.

Edward scowled, removed his shoe and dropped it next to the dog lying on the rug. Heidi yelped and ran to Naomi.

"*Edward!*" Naomi reprimanded him for his carelessness.

"It never touched her," he shot back. "*Females,*" he mumbled under his breath.

Chapter VII

"Disclosure"

"Clean hands are better than full ones
in the sight of God."

—Publilius Syrus

The next evening, Hiram anxiously dressed for the seven-thirty dinner engagement at Brachney Hall. He was exhausted and in ill spirits. Earlier that afternoon, on completion of his chores, he got word that a henhouse roof failed in the late afternoon rain; Mrs. Garber's chickens had escaped, running wild.

Hiram recalled the incident, which involved mud, two dozen fearful, cackling chickens and the neighbor's hungry dog. He pulled on the second boot, dreading the journey to Brachney Hall, albeit it only a brief ride. He was not sure if the day's tasks or the anxiety of possibly failing again with Livia, was enticing him to fall back onto the bed and to go to sleep.

He left his estate with little hope, patience, or energy and arrived at Brachney Hall a quarter hour earlier than Livia. He sat with Edward in the drawing room. Too tired to pace, Hiram waited anxiously, flipping through a half dozen copies of *The Pall Mall Magazine*, until Livia entered with Naomi.

"Good evening, Hiram," Livia said, wearing a forgiving smile and one of the most attractive dresses that he had ever seen. He stood, blank-faced before her.

"Hiram?"

"Livy, you look exquisite."

"Thank you. You look quite handsome, as well."

Naomi smiled.

Edward rolled his eyes. "Shall we play a hand of pinochle before we dine?"

Naomi cut in, "No, no, we do not have time for that. Come sit by Hiram on the couch, Livia." Naomi took the rocking chair. "Livia, how have you been in that *tiny* room?"

Hiram looked away.

Livia replied, "Well, it is certainly a pleasure to come here to your lovely home. It is a bit boring there."

"I cannot imagine how *lonely* you must be and how *dangerous* it is living directly above all those drunkards," Naomi added, glaring at Hiram.

Hiram slapped his hands against his thighs and stood up with objection. "Naomi, I should like to assist you in the kitchen," he demanded, taking her arm.

Edward sat back, tongue in cheek, believing that his wife deserved his nephew's expected censure.

Livia twisted the leather handles of her pocketbook. "Lovely evening."

Edward moved to the rocking chair. "Aye. Was it a pleasurable ride from the village?"

"Yes—cooler than last evening."

Edward nodded. "Prepared for Parents' Night?"

"I believe so. I have something that I wanted to ask you about," she said, opening her purse and removing an envelope. "Being the expert that you are, could you please, tell me what the tiny words on the stamp mean?"

Oh no. He closed his eyes, knowing that they would fail him.

While the master of Brachney Hall was fighting his vision problem, the mistress was the subject of Hiram's inquisition.

"Naomi, why did you invite me? To humiliate me?"

"Hiram, I was merely making small talk with Livia. But now, that you mention it, Livia should not be subject to such horrid living arrangements."

"Do you think that I banished her? I tell you, she left on her own accord!"

"Might I inquire as to what could have possibly driven her to such a desperate decision?"

"Not that it is any of your business, but Miss Nichols left because she found my aversion to men courting her while she was living in my house to be unacceptable!"

"You are not yet married. And *please*, lower your voice. Now, clarify your meaning of 'courting'."

"Gifts—gifts from all over the world on my doorstep! Gifts from men that are well aware that she belongs to me!" He threw up his arms and began pacing.

"*Really* Hiram, a few harmless gifts? Livia loves you. An entire carriage of gold could not change that."

Hiram stopped, still scowling.

"Hiram, these simple tokens mean nothing more to her than objects of art. Rest assured that her heart belongs to you. Feel confident that you may trust her. Livia would never hurt you...as I did."

He turned away. His wavering confidence being tested, he returned to that familiar spot where logic and reason were lost; fear reigned superior. Naomi recognized the symptoms and took his hand. "Hiram do not let the past cloud your thoughts. This is Livia—the woman whom God has sent to share your life."

Hiram folded his arms across his chest.

"Trust in her. You have no other choice; she *is*

your life."

When they returned to the drawing room, Edward and Livia were standing above the lamp discussing the stamp.

"Are you sure Edward? I think those are numbers," Livia said quizzically.

Naomi identified the problem instantly. "Maybe *I* should take a look," Naomi said in frustration with her stubborn husband.

"Never mind, Naomi. You do not know Russian. I will get my lens after dinner," Edward said indignantly.

Naomi turned to Hiram, "Are all the McDonnally men, so incredibly stubborn in their refusal to wear eyeglasses?"

Hiram's gaze did not leave the inviting eyes of Miss Nichols when he replied.

"Eyeglasses are a sign of weakness—so my father professed, as did Grandfather," Hiram mumbled.

Naomi sat down across from Edward. "With no disrespect, that opinion is purely primitive. Anyone who does not take advantage of an opportunity to improve his life is nothing less than foolish."

Hiram ignored her comment and looked down at Livia's fingers still holding the envelope. "What is that?"

"An envelope. I asked Edward about the stamp," her voice quavered.

"One of your father's past letters?" Hiram asked.

"No." Her brief answer brought silence to the room.

"Did you say the stamp was Russian?" Hiram forced a smile.

"Aye," Edward confirmed.

"Russia." Hiram left the divan and walked a few steps away. He turned wearing an expression of one armed and ready to face his opponent. "The letter is from Russia, Livy?"

"Yes," Livia said quietly.

"From whom?" Hiram's brows knitted.

Livia's hand moved to her forehead. "Naomi, Edward, I have seemed to have developed a frightful headache. Would you mind if I declined your dinner invitation?"

Before either had a chance to respond, Hiram did. "I mind!"

Within seconds, Hiram was offering apologies to the disappointed hosts and escorting Livia to *his* carriage in the drive.

Hiram sat in the only chair in Livia's room above the pub. The empty envelope bearing the Russian stamp was crushed in his fist.

"Everything, Livy. All of it!" he demanded.

Livia went to work removing items from the drawers of the paint-chipped bureau. The accumulation of "gifts" began small: a shawl, two hats, a picture frame, and a pocketbook.

Hiram watched in horror as the pile grew: six scarves, a fur cape, a golden looking glass, two pair of gloves, a teapot, about a dozen handkerchiefs, and three bottles of French perfume. Livia paused with a quizzical look. She dumped the jewelry from her box to the bed, and then tossed it on top of the cape. Hiram ran his hand across his beard anxiously while she added a hand mirror with comb and brush set from atop the bureau. She then emptied the dresses from the wardrobe an explained, "These were originals designed by a sister of one of my *friends."*

He shifted uncomfortably. She then pulled out the travel bags from beneath the bed and tossed them on the pile. She gave her hands a brush together in her final check of the room. "Oh," she sighed.

Hiram's eyes widened as she removed her coat, and added it to the mound. She then pushed the pile back to give her room to sit on the edge of the bed. She then removed her shoes and tossed them over her shoulder to the mountain of "misappropriated" gifts. "One evening at the theatre, the strap broke on my left shoe. These were appreciated replacements."

She left the bed and approached him. She turned her back to him.

"Could you please help me with the buttons? The dress was a Christmas present from Benjamin's Nana."

Hiram was speechless. He looked at the mammoth collection stacked on the bed, then at her dress. "As much as I detest the dress, you can dispose of it, after we return home."

"Very well. Excuse me." Livia said, pulling the pillowcase from her pillow and discreetly stuffed her lingerie inside. For this Hiram was grateful.

"I am ready," she announced.

Hiram slowly opened his clenched fist revealing the source of this madness, and tossed the envelope to crown his success. He removed his jacket and helped her put it on, but had to struggle to maintain a serious expression in seeing her comical appearance donning the enormous coat. He picked up his barefoot reward and carried her down to the carriage.

***

The following morning, Hiram opened his bedroom door and found the "dress" in question folded neatly on top of his jacket, lying on the hall floor. He placed the dress on the hall table and shook out his jacket when a piece of paper fluttered to the carpet. He picked it up and smiled as he read:

> *Darling, I adore my dala haus.*
> *It is beautiful! Thank you!*

"Oh Livy, if you liked it, you will be thrilled with your real gift," he mumbled. He slipped on his jacket, taking note that his pocket was empty. *Aye she adored the carved horse.*

He carried the dress down to the kitchen and tossed it onto the table. "Good morning, Eloise."

"Good morning, sir."

"Please dispose of this frock."

Eloise picked up the dress and shook it out. "But sir, it is much too elegant to toss in the—" She stopped, holding her tongue.

"Very well, donate it to the less fortunate."

"Yes, sir. Breakfast will be served shortly."

"Thank you. I will be in my study."

Hiram met Livia, wearing one of Sophia's dresses, at the end of the corridor. He grabbed her arm and pulled her into the study.

"Mr. McDonnally!"

"Kiss me you impoverished wench and I shall purchase you a wardrobe finer than that of the Duchess of Roxburghe!"

She looked up, close in his embrace, "And what do you know of the fineries of the Duchess?"

"Before you and I met, the engaging Miss Goelet paid our fair isle a visit. Had the millionairess met yours truly, she may have not settled for the Duke. Aye, 'tis a pity that she is the mistress of such a quaint estate."

"Their estate on the border—*quaint?*"

"Aye."

"But my father said Floors Castle was situated on nearly seven-hundred thousand acres."

"Aye, as I said—quaint."

Hiram could wait no longer and kissed her passionately.

Livia caught her breath. "Hiram, might I ask how large is this estate?"

"As I said, the Roxburghe estate is quaint."

Livia raised her brows and swallowed.

"Since you so graciously obliged my request, I will replenish your wardrobe. Where did you get that frock?"

"Sophia." Livia rolled her eyes. "Hiram, I know that it is not my business, but what *did* Avera do to Delilah?"

"After the trial, I sent Delilah a wire. She is fine, but she had to postpone her wedding. Avera destroyed her gown. That is why I never received an invitation. She assures me that it will be rescheduled when her fiancé returns from his tour of duty."

"That is so sad."

"Aye, but perhaps for the best. Now, my love, if you will excuse me I have a contract to examine before breakfast."

He took a seat at his desk where he removed a short stack of papers from the top drawer and began reading. Livia gazed at the hundreds of books neatly arranged in the oak shelving, covering the walls. "I would venture to guess that those on the top shelves are feeling neglected and insignificant."

Hiram turned to her. "Neglected and insignificant?"

Livia shrugged.

"Be my guest; give them a reason to live," he said grinning, and returned to his papers.

Livia gingerly wheeled the ladder to the shelf displaying two particularly interesting candidates: Tolstoy's *Anna Karenina* and H.G Well's *Time Machine*. A third caught her eye. *Oh, this is supposed to be hilarious,* she thought smiling down on the copy of Grossmith's *Diary of a Nobody*. She slowly ascended the ladder, removed the three, one-by-one, and tucked them in the crux of her arm. She backed down the ladder inching her grip with the free hand.

"Good grief, woman!" Hiram rushed to her and reached up. "Hand me those books and use both hands."

"Thank you."

Hiram placed them on the table, gave her a look of disapproval for her carelessness, and returned to his work. Livia sat down in the "nook" and examined the three volumes. She chose the third and frowned slightly in attempting to open the cover. She then realized that the pages were not pages and the book not a book, but a box made to look like one. *I have heard of these.* Livia glanced up at Hiram, who was sitting with his back to her. She tried opening what appeared to be the lid of the "book." It did not open at first. She felt around the perimeter and discovered a tiny latch beneath the back edge. She was holding it up when Eloise arrived.

"Breakfast is served, Master, Miss Nichols," Eloise announced.

Hiram replied, without looking up, "One moment, Eloise, I need to finish reading this page."

"Yes, sir." Eloise disappeared and Livia quickly slid the mysterious box beneath the other two novels on the table.

The morning meal, Eloise's Thursday morning specialty of German cuisine, was unanimously voted to be extraordinarily delicious.

As they finished, Hiram explained, "Livia, Rahzvon is handling the farms. I shall be back at four for tea. Daniel and I are meeting with Guillaume to discuss some renovations for the new store. I understand that your school is closed for the day."

"Yes, one of the children is having a birthday picnic at their home and I can use the time to finalize the details for tonight."

"Tonight?"

"Parents' Night, remember?"

"Ah…aye. Very well. Stay and finish your tea. I need to get going." He leaned down to kiss the top of her head and squeezed her shoulder. "Good day, Love, everyone."

Livia finished her tea and returned to Hiram's study. She closed the doors and hurried to retrieve the curious book. She removed the concealing volumes and carried the box over to the window seat. She fiddled with the latch until the lid opened.

"Ohh." She laid the box open on the desk. Something wrapped in brown paper lay inside. She stared at it momentarily. *I should not be doing this. I am not even a family member, as yet.* She closed the lid and stepped back, thinking that it could be important—something that was lost and needed to be found. She inched her way back to the desk and casually ran her fingers to the lid edge. She dare not. She withdrew her hand. She folded her arms, staring at the box. It was hidden, obviously. For a reason, but what reason? She began pacing, struggling with her unrelenting conscience.

Finally, she could stand it no longer and returned to the desk. She opened the lid. Her fingers crept to the brown paper. She gently pressed on it. She looked to the door, then to the window, and lifted the package from the box. She carefully unfolded the paper, finding nothing more than a pair of gold-rimmed spectacles and a doctor's receipt.

With a knowing smile she commented, "That old fraud. So no McDonnally men need spectacles?" She wrapped them in the paper and was about to return them to the box when she noticed a label on the underside of the paper. *Deliver to Mr. Geoffrey McDonnally,* she read. "Mr. McDonnally your secret has been discovered," she laughed. "A weakness, eh?"

Livia's first instinct was to share her discovery with Naomi, to help convince Edward that at least one McDonnally male wore eyeglasses—his hypocritical brother, no less, thus releasing Edward from his shame of needing them. However, this would require a confession to her snooping. She wrapped the glasses and started to replace them in the box, when she saw it. She placed the glasses on the table and held the box up to the light. A slip of paper was glued inside the bottom of the box.

Chapter VIII

"Linoleum?"

"The very tones in which we spake
Had something strange,
I could not mark:
The leaves leaves of memory seemed to make
A mournful rustling in the dark."

—Henry W. Longfellow

Having already violated Geoffrey's privacy, Livia saw no harm in completing the deplorable deed. She gently tugged on the paper to remove it from the bottom of the box. *Good glue, Geoffrey.* She grimaced as it tore slightly with the final pull.

Livia turned over the slip of paper and read the name inked across it.

Calvin Quinn—Exeter

Calvin Quinn? The name was not that of the physician who had prescribed the spectacles. Who was this? She knew that it had to be someone of significance to be so carefully hidden from view by such elaborate means. But why?

She stared blankly at the name. Dare she tell Hiram? Yet, another skeleton in the McDonnally closet? She saw the repercussions of Rahzvon's discovery of Avera's note. Her head began to spin with indecision. She had to tell someone. How could she keep this intriguing information to herself?

She memorized the name, returned the paper and packaged glasses back to the box, and closed the cover. She carried it back to the ladder and returned it to its rightful place on the top shelf. Her earlier excitement at the find was now lost to guilt, confusion, and desperation. In leaving the study, she sought solace in a turn about the extensive grounds.

Calvin Quinn? Who was he? She considered confiding in Rahzvon as he did her, but knew Sophia would throw a fit.

She considered the name "Quinn" as a middle or surname, but decided that it was undoubtedly the latter. Perhaps he was a friend of Geoffrey's or a relative—maybe an enemy or simply the previous owner of the fake book box. She thought that if he were a relative, his name would appear in the family Bible. The unknowns taunted her for the rest of the day. She made her way to the west wing, completed her tasks, and posted a welcome sign on the door for the attending parents.

When Hiram returned, Livia joined him for tea. While he was cleaning up at the kitchen basin she teased, "My Mr. McDonnally whose sheep or chickens did you rescue today?"

"Your Mr. McDonnally spent several hours this morning, delivering twin lambs. I sent for Edward to help." He dried his hands.

"Do you realize that you are probably the only man of your position who looks like this daily?" Livia smiled.

"We are all equal in God's eyes," Hiram said nonchalantly, dropping the towel to the table.

Livia picked it up and hung it on the rack. "Well said. Now come tell me all about it. Eloise has tea prepared in the garden."

"The details would not lend to a pleasant dining experience, Livy." He opened the back door for her.

"I see." She sat in the chair he offered and spread her napkin across her lap. "Since, you seem to be in a religious mood, might I ask, was your mother a very religious woman? I know that your grandmother, Sarah, was known for her piety."

"Somewhat," Hiram said, and then sipped the hot soup.

"Did Amanda keep a family Bible?"

"She did." He tore a piece of bread from the

loaf.

"I have never seen it."

Hiram placed a slice of caboc cheese on his bread. "Ah, that reminds me. I need to make a new entry in the family tree."

"Oh, Hiram," she said sheepishly. "Is it not customary to wait until after the wedding?"

Hiram looked at her quizzically and then grinned. "Aye, it is love, and Mr. and Mrs. Sierzik have been married for some time, now."

"Of course." Livia blushed and looked out at the blooming rhododendron. "The blooms are profuse this summer."

"They are every summer." He grinned and sipped his tea.

"When will you think that you will be entering Rahzvon's name?" she asked casually.

"Livy, if you would like to see the Bible, you need only ask."

"If I would not be intruding," she said meekly. She could not believe that she said that. Her innocent? Hardly.

"I will even show you where your name will be written before too long."

Livia smiled. *Before too long?* How much longer could it be?

After they finished, Hiram left Livia in the parlor and went to change his clothing. Livia paced around the room. *I may need to scan quickly for the Quinn name. I will ask many questions to allow for extra time. Oh dear, what if the tree extends over several pages?*

Hiram entered the parlor carrying the large leather bound Bible. "Here it is. It is several hundred years old."

Livia followed to the table where he sat and

removed the pen and jar of ink from the drawer.

Over Hiram's shoulder, she began the search. Nothing on that page. Hiram registered Rahzvon's first name next to Sophia's and paused. He looked up at Livia. "You know, I do not know what Rahzvon's middle name is—if he has one."

"Manstrong," Livia uttered, pouring carefully over the page.

"What did you say?"

"Manstrong—his name is *Manstrong*, Hiram."

"Very amusing, Livy. Did Sophia tell you that?" he chuckled.

Livia looked up at his skeptical grin. "I am serious, that is his middle name. And no, she did not tell me. Sophia does not know," she said, reaching over and flipping back a page.

"Then how is it that you came to this discovery?" Hiram's forehead wrinkled.

"Rahzvon told me." Livia, reached down to turn the last page.

Hiram squinted suspiciously at her, still holding his pen poised to sign.

Livia shook her head when she did not locate the Quinn name. "Are you not going to enter it?"

Hiram looked back to the book, which was now open to a different page.

"Here," she said, turning back to the line for Rahzvon's name.

Hiram glanced up to her innocent grin and placed the pen on the line. "I suppose it is Gisaleon, I do not know how to spell it."

"Oh no, it is the name his mother created. Man-strong, just as it sounds. The story is that she knew from the moment he was born that he would someday be a fine, strong man. Of course, Strongman Sierzik would have been a bit too much, so she reversed it."

"Of course." Hiram painfully added it to the register; it was like admitting Rahzvon's superior strength and power. Annoyed at Livia's private conversation with Rahzvon and the name in general, he quickly added the Sierzik name, blotted it, and slammed the book closed. "I have paperwork waiting. I shall see you later."

He left Livia preoccupied with the Quinn mystery and unconcerned with his momentary jealousy. She needed to speak with Naomi; she solved mysteries, Sophia had said.

"Oh, Hiram! Might we invite Naomi and Edward for dinner? Rahzvon and Sophia are dining with Allison and Guillaume."

"Sorry to hear it. I am certain you are disappointed," he uttered.

This comment confused her, but she ignored it and continued with her inquiry.

"Do you mind? It will be at, about eight."

"Why so late?"

"Parents' Night, remember?"

"Nay...uh, aye, tell Eloise to prepare something—anything. Why the invitation?"

"I want Naomi's opinion on the linoleum pattern for the kitchen floor."

"Sounds fascinating," he said, closing the pocket doors behind him and mumbling, "Manstrong—ridiculous."

Livia knocked at the doors.

"Come in," Hiram said, spreading the papers over his desk.

"Hiram, what would you say to me taking a little trip to...Kilcaldy."

Hiram turned. "Kilcaldy? The linoleum factory?" he chuckled. "Livy if you need it checked out, I can send a man."

"Well, actually, I wanted to examine their samples."

"Nonsense, I can have samples delivered."

"Oh."

Hiram spun around toward her, "Livy, tell me that Benjamin is not residing in Kilcaldy."

"No, no, Hiram."

"Then who?"

"The factory, of course."

"Livy, I have to look over this proposal." He turned back to his work.

"Yes, dear."

She walked up behind him. "The Cox Brothers?"

"They own a jute factory in Lochee."

"Oh, that is nice."

"It is the largest in the world."

"Ohh."

Hiram lowered the forms that he held and looked over his shoulder. "Livy, is there not something that you need to prepare for your Children's Night?"

"No and it is *Parents'* Night." Livia backed away and Hiram continued reading.

He soon felt a tap on his shoulder. He sighed and turned to her. "What is on your mind, Livy?"

"A brief trip."

"To Kilcaldy."

"No, Exeter."

"Exeter?" He dropped the papers to the desk. "Good grief, woman! Do you have any idea how far it is to Exeter? And why Exeter?"

"It is in England," she said nervously.

"Not only is it in Devin, but the southernmost region of Britain. Why on earth would you want to go there?"

Livia turned away. "It is not important—only a passing notion."

Hiram returned to the proposals, "I recommend that you let it pass and do not mention it again."

"And if I did?" she said just above a whisper.

Hiram began tapping his fingers on the desk. "Did what, Livy?"

"Mention it, again."

Hiram rested his head in his hands in frustration. "If you so desire—go to Kilcaldy—go to Exeter—go to Dublin—go to America. But *please*, leave me to my work."

She had crossed the line and had made him angry. That was not her intent.

"Hiram?"

"Livy, please! I have very little time!"

Livia quickly left the study, regretting her tactics to make the research trip to investigate the Quinn name. Hiram, too, lamenting his abruptness with her, swept the papers from the desk, and shoved his chair back. He got up and began to pace. *Exeter?*

He went to look for Livia and found her with very little effort, as she was sitting on the window seat in the parlor. She did not acknowledge his entry when he took a chair by the hearth.

After a minute of deliberation, he spoke to her, "Livy."

"Yes."

"Would you care to enlighten me as to your intentions for travelling to Exeter?"

"No."

Taken aback by her bluntness, although familiar with the response, he tried to remain collected and cool.

"If it is really that important to you, perhaps I should accompany you there. Would that be favorable?"

"No."

With that, he abruptly left his chair to confront his offender.

"Livy, I have hours of work to accomplish in half the time. I will not devote any more discussion in deciphering your mysterious behavior. But, I am going to ask you one more time and then I shall never mention it again. Who lives in Exeter?"

"Many people, I am certain."

"You know what I mean. Who is it this time?"

Livia's jaw dropped. "Ah!" She left the seat and walked across the room. She turned and said in a fierce whisper, "Is it not enough that you have disposed of nearly all my possessions, including the very dress off my back? Now, I am bullied into surrendering my every thought? Mr. McDonnally, I am a private person. I treasure my privacy!"

"Hah! Public authoress of the years, do not talk to me of such absurdities. You not only took the pleasure in sharing your most private thoughts with the entire world, but you exploited mine, as well—not only on the printed page, but in plays all over the universe!"

She boldly stepped toward him and stared up into his frustrated eyes.

"Are we having a disagreement?" she asked casually.

He squinted. "What did you say?"

"I asked if we are engaged in a disagreement."

"I thought that is what you said. I believe we are."

"Does it not seem peculiar that two people

who are bound by their eternal love should be having a great number of disagreements?"

Hiram cleared his throat and loosened his collar. He shifted his weight and folded his arms across his chest. She waited for his response. He finally replied.

"People in love...together...need to have a fair number of discussions prior to their marriage," he said as profoundly as possible.

"You are probably right." She gave a little laugh. "What am I saying? Of course, you are always right and as you said, you shall never mention it again." She smiled sweetly. "Now, go along, return to your work." She grasped his arm and gave him a gentle push toward the archway. Hiram turned from the hall to see her genuine smile and little wave.

He walked slowly across the hall to his desk and pulled out the chair thinking, *she did it again.* He sat down and stroked his beard looking toward the hall. *Extraordinary. She is a genius or I am a fool.* She was a genius.

That evening, Hiram kept a close eye on Livia and Naomi. Their earlier conversation of Livia's successful school event had ended and there seemed to be something unsavory brewing between them. It was obvious as they abruptly ended their conversation when he returned to the parlor with Edward who had joined him for a few minutes of night air in the garden. Their female expressions were not indicative of women caught in idle gossip and their inexplicable "sudden" alliance had not developed solely from the monumental decision in linoleum patterns. Naomi did her utter best to convince Hiram that it was.

"Livia, perhaps Hiram will consider having linoleum installed in the kitchen of your school. It provides an excellent surface for a hasty cleanup."

The women looked to him for his approval.

He snickered, "Perhaps I should consider covering the entire west wing, walls included."

Flags went up when Livia ignored his reply and requested that Naomi accompany her to the main kitchen to consider color and size for the flooring.

He started to follow them, when Edward teased, "Man, do not tell me you desire input for that delicate decision?"

Hiram hesitated and resumed his seat. "They are up to something," he said, rubbing his palms together, staring blankly.

"It is only linoleum—the rage. Are you concerned that she is going to remodel the entire house?"

"Nay, I have been watching them. There is a secret between them; something they are concealing."

Edward's face brightened, "Our child! Naomi may be with child!"

"Nay, Edward. It is Livy."

"Hiram, NO!" Edward said with shock and disapproval.

"Not that. What do you take me for? Nay, there is someone—someone she needs to meet with before it is too late."

"Too late for what? There you go again. You really need to stop dwelling on the past. The woman is devoted to you."

"You have no idea of the multitude of men that are devoted to *her*," Hiram scoffed.

"What has driven you to this paranoia?"

"Her desire to go *alone* to Exeter."

"Exeter?"

"She refuses to offer, or should I say, cleverly avoids any explanation."

"Perhaps, she is planning a surprise for you."

"That is what I fear. The last surprise made himself up to look like me and used my name."

"That was for a play production," Edward grinned. His expression turned to one of concern for his pacing nephew. "You should feel honored. There are no plays or novels depicting my character."

Hiram stopped and rolled his eyes.

In the kitchen, Livia hustled Naomi back into the maid's room and explained, "Quickly, I have something that I must ask you."

"About the flooring?"

"No, about the McDonnallys."

"What is it?"

"Are you familiar with a clan member of the name, Calvin Quinn? I checked the family Bible. It is not there."

"I have never heard the name. Who is he?"

"Well," Livia wiped the perspiration from her hands on her skirt, "I feel a bit unhinged about confiding this, but I discovered the name glued inside a box—actually a box that is made to look like a book. I found it purely by accident on the top shelf in the study. I have not told Hiram about it."

"Oh?" Naomi's eyes widened with interest.

"It was Hiram's father's box. I know this because it also contained a pair of eyeglasses prescribed to him."

"Ah! That old hypocrite! Edward is straining

his eyes because of his brother's silly remarks and he had spectacles?"

"Now, we have no proof that he wore them. The doctor may have prescribed them and he refused."

"I am certain that he did wear them—in the secret confines of his study! I am appalled. For what other reason would he keep them hidden where no one could find them? If he refused to wear them he would have disposed of them."

Livia cocked her head. "You are *very* good at solving mysteries, as Sophia said." She smiled at Naomi. "You are another Sherlock Holmes."

Naomi smiled humbly, "Edward is always saying that, too. What about the *name* in the box?"

"You are the expert so I am consulting with you. The name was followed by 'Exeter'."

"You said 'glued in the box'?"

"Yes, on a slip of paper."

"So that it would not be lost or revealed when the box was opened."

"Excellent, Naomi!"

"Thank you. Exeter, hmm? That must have been his residence—where he could be located, if need be."

"Do you think that he is connected with the spectacles? Another physician's name was on the bill of sale."

"Perhaps, but I doubt it." Naomi tapped her fingers on her lips, pondering. "This box was a secret chest of sorts where things could be stored. I believe that this Calvin chap is someone that Geoffrey dare not forget and needed a record of his location; the identity of a man that he dare not reveal for public scrutiny or entrust to another living soul."

The two women stared pensively at one another, and then said in unison, "We have to go to Exeter."

"Hiram does not relish the idea of me going there. I already inquired. He is terribly suspicious."

"Of course. We will have to hire my detective to go," Naomi said steepling her closed hands. "We shall have the information quickly—within a few days."

Livia nodded with approval.

"It may be of little significance, but worth the research, Livia."

"I did not share the information with Hiram, because of the eyeglass issue."

"I understand; pride in the McDonnally men runs as deep as their dimples. One has to be very cautious in addressing it."

"What if this Calvin Quinn is yet another skeleton in the McDonnally closet? The episode with Avera nearly killed me."

"Once we have the facts, we will examine the issue with prudence, before revealing Quinn to Edward and Hiram."

At that moment, Edward and Hiram entered the kitchen, unnoticed.

Naomi continued, "For now, his identity will be strictly between you and—"

Naomi's head rose with a start, seeing the two intruders before them.

Chapter IX

"Groundbreaking"

"Beware of the wolf in sheep's clothing."

—Holy Bible

Naomi swallowed, *"Edward,"* she said casually. Livia fearfully risked a glimpse at the condemning glare of her intended.

"*'His'* identity?" Hiram reproached.

Livia looked helplessly to her accomplice when Naomi put a protective arm around Livia's waist. "Do not fret, Livia. I shan't let them ruin your surprise." She took Livia's hand and pulled her hurriedly past, toward the hall.

"Did I not tell you it was a surprise?" Edward gloated.

Hiram looked to the empty corridor and shook his head and stroked his beard, "Nay, I do not believe it."

Not another word of Exeter was mentioned. Hiram continued with his daily routine, beginning each day on a milking stool and ending it falling asleep on the desk chair. His dark eyes lost their luster and an affliction of coughing and sneezing spells wore him down. Despite the increased necessity for energy to sustain him, his appetite diminished. The "burning of the candle at both ends" unfortunately had taken its toll on the groundbreaking day of Daniel and Beatrice's new shop.

The crowd of interested villagers waited patiently for the honorary benefactor at the site of the new venture. Twenty minutes passed before Daniel grew concerned; it was not in Hiram's character to be late for such an important engagement, nor any appointment, for that matter. Rahzvon volunteered to ride back to the estate to see what was delaying Hiram.

"I should go with you," Livia insisted.

"No, I am sure that he is only running late.

We will be back soon."

Livia agreed but began imagining the worst—not Hiram's health, but the possible visit of one of her past suitors. *Oh no, I hope it is not Benjamin.*

When Rahzvon arrived, he found the servant, Roy, in a panic in the study.

"Am I glad to see you, Mr. Sierzik. Mr. McDonnally is ill."

Breathing laboriously, Hiram lay slumped over the desk. Rahzvon could see the beads of perspiration on Hiram's face.

"Hiram?" Rahzvon touched his shoulder.

"Sir, I think that he is unconscious."

"Quick, Roy, help me get him to the parlor, then send someone to fetch Dr. Lambert and the family. He is at the village waiting with the others."

Hiram lay in his bed with Livia sitting at his side.

"How is he?" Livia asked.

Dr. Lambert tucked his stethoscope into his bag. "He is sufferin', Miss, but his chances are good; he comes from hearty stock. But, this life-style, workin' nearly twenty hours a day, may be helpin' the community, but 'tis threatenin' the man's life. His exhaustion has put him at risk for more ailments than I care to mention. At this point, he canna fight off the simplest o' colds."

"I know. The coughing has been incessant. I should have done more to make him rest."

"Dunna blame yerself; Hiram's a stubborn, powerful man, who has been brought to his knees by his own charitable doin's. He is nigh on to developin' pneumonia. He needs to rest, not that he could do much else at this point, and plenty o' food, as well. He has lost entirely too much weight o'er the last few months."

"He has been too tired to take his evening meal," Livia sniffled, wiping the tear that trickled down her cheek.

"There now, ye need to be strong for him. Ye hae to keep him restin' for at least a fortnight. It shan't be easy, because he will feel like resumin' his charity work. Once he's regained his strength, he canna return until all symptoms o' the cold hae subsided. I demand it. It takes a great deal to bring down a man o' his stature; this is proof o' the seriousness of his condition. He's to be quarantined from anyone wit' any illness. Now, dunna over do. Remember that Hiram has a capable staff."

"Yes, sir."

"Now, I shall leave you with this essence of cinnamon and quinine for his cold and influenza. I'll explain his condition to his kin."

"Thank you."

"Yer welcome." He stopped in the doorway. "If ye love him, and ye do, ye shall make him behave. I dunna care how ye do it."

"I will."

"If he doesna show any sign o' improvement in the course o' the next three days, fetch me. Good evenin' Miss Nichols."

"Good evening, Doctor Lambert."

The news of Hiram's condition was not well received. Edward regretted his impatience with Hiram's proofreading of their contracts; Rahzvon lamented his inability to assist with the past farm work, as his hands were not quite healed. Hannah's stoic nature relented to one of fearful despair and Naomi's latent feelings of concern for her past love, emerged in forms of short-tempered outbreaks and occasional, discreet, tearful breakdowns. Although, she was very much in love with Edward, the thought of life without Hiram's presence was unbearable. He had been part of her life for as long as she could remember. Naomi, like Sophia in her fragile state, gave way to many emotional outbursts.

To everyone's fear and disappointment, Hiram did not improve over the three-day period. The doctor returned and offered little encouragement. He had done all that he could. Naomi and the religious members of the family turned to prayer; those not so pious, did the same, as they grasped for any viable alternative to help the man they loved so dearly.

The fifth night the vigilant group congregated in the parlor catching a few moments of sleep, while they waited with hopes that the Almighty had chosen to spare Hiram's life.

Livia, trembling, lay on top the covers curled next to him. Memories of her past with him drifted in and out of her thoughts: Hiram was standing behind the counter in the clock shop. He looked up at her with those twinkling black eyes and then he smiled. She could barely breathe; her heart skipped a beat. Years later at the convention: he climbed into the carriage next to her. Her heart nearly stopped that time. He was so intimidating, yet he could not conceal his sweet shyness. The charade in his study: strong and confident, he carried her like a delicate statue from the desk to the divan. He was always smiling, strong, and healthy. Now he was weak and helpless, fighting for his next breath. She scooted closer to him and wept with visions of Hiram walking the floor with Kade, as she fell asleep.

The next morning Hiram opened his eyes. He squinted, focusing on the stream of dawning light that crept between the parted curtains. He looked down to Livia's arm lying across his chest and smiled weakly. He raised his hand to touch her face, but the weight of his arm deterred him.

"Livy," he whispered.

Livia stirred but continued sleeping. He closed his eyes and fell back into a deep sleep that lasted nearly a full day.

The next time he wakened, his eyes opened to greet Livia's astonished expression and a tearful welcome. After a lengthy embrace, she asked, blotting her cheeks. "Darling, how do you feel?"

"Like I have been drinking scotch for a month of Sundays. What happened, Livy?"

"You passed out from exhaustion on the day of the groundbreaking ceremony."

"Oh, *not* the ceremony."

"Daniel and Beatrice understand. We have all been worried out of our minds. Do you think you could eat something?"

"Tell Eloise, to empty the pantry, I would go down for breakfast, if these tired limbs would cooperate."

"It is just as well. The doctor left strict orders that you are to remain here for the next two weeks, at the very least."

"Livy, no one orders me." He coughed.

"Very well, do not think of them as orders, but rather *suggestions* to extend your life into the next month."

"Next month?" he asked groggily.

"We nearly lost you. Now enjoy your holiday and do what you are told."

"What is the state of the war?"

"The Germans have taken Brussels and the Emperor of Japan has declared war on Germany, as well."

Hiram closed his eyes in hearing the ominous report. "I need only a couple days rest; there are people who depend on me and the staff."

"Rahzvon assures me that if he wears a good pair of leather gloves, now, he can easily replace you."

Hiram scowled. *Manstrong.* "You tell Mr. Sierzik that he is to report to me every day before going out."

Livia tightened her lips, concealing her smile. "Of course, darling, I am certain that he will be in need of instruction."

Hiram gave a sharp nod of confirmation. "I need my paperwork from my desk."

"That is not necessary; Mr. Raheleka and Gaelon are helping Edward sort out all of that."

"Gaelon? Thank God he got safely out of Belgium."

"Yes, he has been flitting back and forth, like a bee to a hive. Now, remain here, I shall tell everyone the good news and order your breakfast."

"Livy, I missed you."

"I know. I really should have come up to see you at least one other time besides this one." She grinned mischievously and left.

Hiram noted the rocking chair positioned next to his bed. The bed pillow lay in the seat. Livia's robe hung across the back. The table beside it was loaded down with Livia's worksheets for her school.

Hannah peeked into the room. "How is my favorite twin?"

"Better. Come on in."

Hannah kissed Hiram's forehead and sat down next to him.

"My dear brother, I have come to greatly admire, Livia."

"Glad to hear it."

"She is an angel. She barely left your side. She has been sleeping in the rocking chair and taking all of her meals here. Sophia and I volunteered to take charge of her school, because she could not bear to leave you."

"There is none like her, Hannah."

"Do not let this one escape or I shall never forgive you. Besides, there is not another woman who could tolerate the McDonnally clan chaos," she laughed.

"She is a saint."

"And you need to rest until your meal is served. Enjoy it and follow the doctor's orders. Not to worry we shan't let you die of boredom," she said, patting his hand.

"Thank you."

"Shh. Close your eyes."

When leaving the room to join the others for breakfast in the dining room, Hannah paused at the top of the staircase. Gaelon was stealthily exiting the study, quietly closing the doors. Hannah froze. Gaelon checked both directions before continuing to the dining room.

Hannah grasped the railing and descended, disturbed by the scene she had witnessed. Something was not right in Gaelon's covert behavior. She slipped through the hall, into the study, and closed the doors behind her in search of some indeterminate evidence of Gaelon's clandestine activity. Nothing appeared to be out of order. Focused on the doors, she inched back toward Hiram's desk. *The drawers should be locked,* she thought, knowing that only Hiram and Edward had keys. Even Gaelon was deprived access, when Edward and Hiram were not present. Her brother was a stickler for guarding his valuable contracts, proposals, and the like. Hannah's hand systematically tugged on each of the brass drawer pulls. The drawers on the right were locked. She knew that locking the middle drawer automatically locked the rest. *The left drawers should be secure, as well.* One last glimpse affirmed that the desktop was clear and there were no papers sitting on any of the tables throughout the room. She glanced at the indifferent bust of Robert Burns positioned on the mantle. *If only you could speak.* She turned to leave, dissatisfied with her failure to disclose any clue to Gaelon's mysterious visit. Abandoning her futile search, she reached for the door to join the others for breakfast. She started to part the doors when a nagging curiosity drew her back to the desk, one more time.

She tried to open the top and middle left drawers with no success. When the bottom left drawer slid open, perspiration formed on her palms. She looked to the door, and then pulled the drawer open wider. On top, there was a large envelope bearing the name of a company that she recognized. She closed the drawer considering the implications of Gaelon's access to the contents. Perhaps, Hiram, in his weakened state, failed to close that drawer when locking the others. *Why was Gaelon violating Hiram's privacy?* Or was he?

How would he have known that the drawer was unlocked? Had he discovered it purely by accident?

She turned to leave when she noted a silhouette of a large form moving away from the cracked door. Someone had been watching her.

In her experience with the café in Paris, Hannah had dealt with her fair share of swindlers, cheaters, and embezzlers. The possibility that Gaelon may be characterized as one of these scoundrels was very disconcerting. Being a strong, independent woman, she had developed her own technique in handling these amoral offenders, but confronting Gaelon, her son-in-law's brother, was another matter. Gaelon was family and more than a casual friend. Now, he may have seen her and realize that she was aware of his possible wrongdoings. She pondered a moment longer before approaching the doors. With her chin up, she entered the hall, confident that she had done nothing wrong; she was not the perpetrator. She rallied her strengths and wits. *I shall not be intimidated, or quick to judge.*

Her unfaltering smile greeted Gaelon, as she entered the dining room. "Good morning, Gaelon, Sophia. Has Rahzvon already left to make the rounds to the farms?"

"Yes, Mama. I am concerned. I certainly do not want my husband falling ill, too, from being overworked," she said, frowning down at two poached eggs staring up at her.

"That will not happen, I assure you, my daughter. We shall combine forces to keep Rahzvon healthy and strong with an abundance of nutritious food and ample rest."

"I am not certain that will be possible. There

is rumor of rationing food."

Hannah spooned out a scoop of marmalade onto her piece of toast. "If so, I am prepared. If there is anyone equipped to cut corners, it is I. I once served eighteen customers with a bag of rice, an onion, a pound of pork and a single turnip.

"Were there any complaints, Mother?"

"I should say not. In fact, many inquired as to when the day's special would be served again. The secret is in the spices."

"Bravo." Gaelon interjected.

Hannah nodded at the compliment. "Sophia, when you find sometime today, I should hope that you would pay your Uncle Hiram a visit. He is nearly ready to fly the coop and would, if his wings were strong enough."

"Certainly, I will challenge him to a game of chess, after I finish my letter to Agnes."

"I thought that you despised the game."

Sophia poked one of the egg eyes with her fork and grimaced. "I do because it is so unnerving—the pressure of feeling backed into a corner with no place to run can be terrifying."

Hannah's gaze moved slowly to the suspect, but Gaelon ignored her attention and turned to Sophia. "Much like the troops. So why torture yourself?"

"The thrill of the hunt, of course."

Hannah teased, "Well, you may have to move his game pieces for him. Now, little mother, your baby is probably screaming in there, hunting for his breakfast," Hannah teased.

"Or *hers*," Sophia suggested.

"Or both," Gaelon chimed in.

Sophia and Hannah exchanged a disapproving look, considering that twin births ran in the McDonnally clan.

After breakfast, Livia met Sophia in the hall on her way to the west wing.

"Going to check if your school is still intact, Professor Nichols?"

Livia smiled. "I am certain that it is in better condition than when I left it. You and your mother have been marvelous. I cannot thank you enough."

"Just promise me that this little future Sierzik, he or she, or both, will replace Joshua as your teacher's pet," Sophia giggled.

"Both?"

"She could be twins!"

"Twins? I never considered the possibility."

"I have to admit, neither did I until Gaelon mentioned it at breakfast. There are several sets in the McDonnally clan." Sophia's jaw dropped. *"Livia!* You, too, may have twins! After you marry, of course."

"Oh dear. Well, your uncle desires six children as a minimum; this would narrow down the time invested." Livia grinned.

"I can imagine three sets of twins running Uncle Hiram ragged—but what a handsome lot they would be."

"Yes, if the women of Scotland fawned over the likes of Zedidiah Hartstrum, imagine when they see my sons."

"A host of Uncle Hirams? I do not think that the world is ready for such a miracle. But they all may drop their guns in awe and the war would be over."

"If that were the case, I would marry your Uncle today.

***

The following day, after having lost the first game, Sophia challenged Hiram to a rematch. Upon entering the hall to the second floor, Eloise caught up to her.

"Miss Sophia," she said, handing her two envelopes. "Please deliver these to the master."

"Of course," she said wearily.

"Another game of chess?"

Sophia nodded.

"Let him win. I shan't care to clean up the disaster, if he loses." Eloise grinned.

"Not to worry." She knocked at the door.

"Come in," Hiram greeted.

"Have your strategies in place, Uncle Hiram?" Sophia asked, entering and placing the chess box on the table next to the bed.

"Aye, always prepared. Good afternoon, Sophia."

"Good afternoon. You really should enjoy the duration of this rest."

"Aye, before returning to the farm work?"

"No. Livia and I were discussing the possibilities of twins in the family—perhaps mine or even yours and Livia's. Can you imagine double sets of your mischievous little McDonnally men?"

"I certainly can and I anticipate the very moment. This old mausoleum has been quiet for much too long. I never realized it until Ka—" Hiram looked away and then smiled at Sophia, "Until visiting Brachney Hall when the Wheaton children were residing there. Seeing their home full of life and energy inspired me to surround myself with a dozen wee glowing faces."

"Having worked in Livia's school, I can assure you that those faces are not always glowing. There will be crying, fighting, screaming, and illness.

Enough to drive you mad!"

"Nothing you can say shall dissuade me; I know what I want." He pointed to the envelopes. "Are those for me?"

She handed them to him. "Yes. One is from America."

"Ah, excuse me for a minute. I have been waiting for this. Go right ahead, set up the board." He opened one of the envelopes. "You know that you are about to lose this game, Mrs. Sierzik." He grinned and looked down at the letter.

"If I lose, it is only because I pity you, Uncle Hiram."

Hiram looked up with a broad smile. "And I shall demand that it was unfair as I am playing one against two."

Sophia smiled and placed two pawns on the board. "Or three."

Hiram did not comment and removed the letter. "Aye, perfect." He grinned and returned the page back to the envelope.

"What is it Uncle?"

"A secret; a surprise for Livy."

"Tell me Uncle! I shan't tell. I promise."

"Nay, I went to too much trouble to work out the details. My plan nearly failed with the war and all. Nay, I shan't tempt you with this one."

Sophia slouched in her chair, pouting.

Hiram opened the second envelope. His pronounced dimples vanished. "Blast it!"

His outburst startled Sophia to the point that she knocked the board from the table. She held her hand to her chest. "Uncle Hiram, what is it?"

"Quickly, Sophia! Out of here! I need to get dressed."

"But Uncle—"

"Now, Sophia! And have a carriage ordered, at once!"

Ignoring her uncle's instructions to order a carriage, Sophia ran from Hiram's room to find Livia.

Frustrated and outraged, Hiram ripped two buttons from his shirt in his rapid dressing.

"I shan't stand for this!"

He pulled on his trousers, buckled his belt and snatched a pair of socks from the bureau.

"Heads will roll—I tell you!"

Steaming from the recent correspondence, Hiram finished dressing and pulled his jacket from the clothes rack on his way out. He jerked open the door which slammed into the plant stand behind it, sending the potted fern to the floor. He charged down the hall like a livid rhinoceros, disregarding everything in his path—which included the maid carrying a stack of freshly laundered linens which toppled to the floor, and a servant picking up the shards of a broken water pitcher.

The stairs creaked under the weight of his heavy footsteps as he descended to the study. He slammed the doors into their pockets and removed the desk key from his breast pocket en route to his desk. He jerked back the chair, sat down and unlocked the central drawer. Reaching down to the bottom left drawer, he snagged every envelope within it and dropped them to the desktop. He spread them around frantically, searching through them. It was gone.

His head spinning with confusion, he anxiously checked and double-checked the labels. Where was it? He removed the contents of every drawer, depositing the unwanted papers wildly to the floor. His black eyes grew darker in his futile efforts. He let out a loud groan of rage and slammed his palms to the desk. He left the study to the main entrance and opened the door when Livia and Sophia ran from the hall.

"What are you doing out of your bed?" Livia asked with alarm.

"Not now, Livy. Sophia where is my carriage?" he reprimanded. "Roy!"

"Uncle Hiram—"

"Not now!"

Chapter X

"Ill-tidings"

"The lip of truth
shall be established forever;
but a lying tongue is but for a moment."

—Holy Bible

The servant appeared seconds later. "Yes, sir?"

"A carriage, now! Make haste!"

Roy ran off and Hiram began pacing in the drive.

Livia called to him, "Hiram, where are you going? I can run any errands that you need. Let me fetch Edward," she begged.

"Not now, Livy—I am thinking!"

There was no doubt as to his anger and despair. He rarely spoke to Livia with such reproof.

"I am going with you!" She ran inside to pull her cardigan from the hall rack and her umbrella from the stand.

Hiram continued pacing, and then stopped. "Where the devil is that carriage? I knew I should have purchased that motorcar."

The clacking of the hooves on the cobblestone drive sent Hiram into a sprint towards the carriage. He flung open the door, as he yelled, "To the telegraph office and quickly!"

"Hiram!" Livia called, running toward him with an outstretched hand. Hiram pulled her into the carriage, which sped off, throwing its passengers back against their seats. Hiram stared blankly at the empty seat across from them. Livia refrained from further inquiry. Concerned with his health, she nervously waited several minutes, before asking, "Are you all right?"

His raging eyes met hers, "Do I look all right? I have never been so outraged in my entire life— and you know how angry I have become." His jaw was set, his teeth clenched—his fits tight on his lap.

Livia closed her eyes, *Please God; tell me that it was not a letter from Benjamin.*

"Whoever is responsible will pay, I can guarantee that. I cannot understand how this occurred, but I shall find out. *No one* crosses a McDonnally without suffering the consequences!"

Relieved that Benjamin was not the object of his anger, Livia still cringed fearfully. She knew Hiram to be fair in his business practices, never ruthless, with exception of the dissolution of Jonathon Turvy's company in vengeance for her abuse. Hiram's wealth was undoubtedly synonymous with great power. She could not imagine who would dare tread on such sacred ground to risk ruination. She concluded that person to be either very foolish or equally powerful.

At McDonnally Manor, Sophia watched Eloise pare potatoes in the kitchen.

"Eloise, do you think Uncle Hiram will have a relapse? He has been in bed for a very long time."

"I would hope not, but I do not doubt it. Dr. Lambert was not satisfied with two weeks of convalescing. He mentioned that the master should rest for at least another week. The influenza nearly killed him."

"He has gone to the telegraph office. There was something dreadful in that letter."

"I regret having delivered it."

"Eloise, neither you, nor I, had a choice in that matter."

Eloise wiped her hands on her apron and patted Sophia's hand. "I pray that he returns quickly and Miss Nichols can convince him to return to his bed. How are you feeling, today?"

"Like an elephant at Regent's Park—tired, fat, but definitely not hungry."

"You may not feel like eating, but you must—a little at a time. Is there anything that I can do for you? Perhaps a magazine picked up from the village."

"No thank you, I have one," she said, glancing at the *Housing Magazine*. "Mother and I are having another knitting session with Aunt Naomi. She says that there is a great deal of relaxation and reward in knitting. I shan't believe that I shall ever learn."

"I can always teach you to crochet, if need be."

"Thank you, I shall keep that option available. Working with one needle has to be easier than two."

"One *hook*."

Sophia dropped the magazine to the table and glanced up at the sound of distant hammering. "They certainly are doing a grand job of repairing the east wing. One would barely believe that it had been in a fire."

"Have you decided which room will be the nursery?"

"Actually, if you promise to keep a secret, Rahzvon is convinced that we shall live in our own home before our baby arrives," Sophia whispered, thumbing through the pages.

"The master is not aware of this?"

Sophia looked up, "No, nor is my mother. We have been trying to squeeze in a search now and again, but have not found anything remotely suitable."

"Be content that you have this wonderful home in the meantime."

"I am, *believe* me."

The grandfather clock struck two times,

sending Sophia from her chair to the hall.

"Good luck with your lesson!" Eloise called.

Sophia nodded, stretched and walked toward the parlor where her mother was reprimanding Roy for assisting in her brother's escape. Roy left without a word in his defense.

"Sophia, I am thoroughly disappointed in that stubborn uncle of yours. He may be brilliant but he does not have a lick of common sense. Insubordinate servants are not helping either. Do you know what inspired your uncle's madness?"

"As a matter of fact, I was the bearer of ill-tidings; I delivered the letter that instigated this uproar. Oh Mother, did you know that Uncle is planning a surprise for Livia?"

"This is about a surprise for Livia?"

"No, that was another letter. But now, with all this bad news, it shall have to wait, I suppose."

"Sophia, what shall have to wait?

"Uncle Hiram's surprise." Sophia balanced the ball of yarn in her hands. "After this, he may go off on a binge and poor Livia may never get her surprise."

"*Sophia!*"

"Well, Mother, it is true. We all know that he has a tendency to take a nip when he is angry and trust me—I was there when he left and he was a mad hatter."

"You speak as if your uncle is a drunkard and you know that is far from the truth. He has only resorted to that irresponsible behavior under severe duress."

"If there was ever an occasion for it, today is it. This is serious, Mother."

Hannah sat down the basket of yarn and slipped the drapery back from the window. "I hope they return soon."

"Mother, Aunt Naomi shan't mind if we forego our knitting lesson. Can we cancel it for today?"

"I suppose. I am not really in the mood, either. I have a great deal on my mind."

"What? Man trouble?"

"No...somewhat."

"Tell me," Sophia whispered behind her hand. "Too many choices—Mr. Raheleka and Gaelon?"

"Never you mind. Now, what shall we do until Naomi arrives?"

"A game of cards. I shall get them." Sophia crossed the hall to the study. "Mama! Come quickly!"

Hannah ran to join Sophia who was standing in awe of the paper-strewn desk and surrounding area. The drawers were all ajar.

"That nip may be closer than we think, Mother."

"What a mess. It is not like him to leave his papers out. It appears that he was looking for some—" Hannah stopped flashing back to the vision of Gaelon leaving Hiram's study.

"I wonder if he found it," Sophia said, squatting to pick up another envelope, as bending was an uncomfortable option.

"We had better leave this cleanup to your uncle. I will have Roy lock the room."

"That is fine with me. I feel like an old woman trying to pick flowers."

"Come along."

Hannah instructed Roy to lock the doors, but felt that it was rather like locking the barn door after the horses escaped. Gaelon's innocence in the matter was highly suspect at this point. The burden of the knowledge of his intrusion weighed heavily upon her.

"I need some air. Sophia, are you up to a turn around the grounds until your aunt Naomi arrives?"

"She is your aunt too, Mama," Sophia giggled.

"*Sophia*, do you want to join me or not?"

"I will get Rusty's leash. I promised Guillaume that I would walk him while he and Allison were out for the day."

"I will meet you in the garden."

Sophia nodded and left.

Hannah turned to Roy, who stepped from the dining room."When Naomi McDonnally arrives, please ask her to meet with me in the garden."

"Yes. Mum."

Peering out the sidelight, Hannah felt certain that Gaelon was involved in Hiram's hasty departure. If Gaelon had stolen from Hiram, she could not tell Sophia, nor warn Rahzvon. She had to tell Hiram. What would he do? She had to speak with Livia first; she would know the best way to handle Hiram. She turned to join Sophia when she saw Gaelon standing before her.

"Hannah, I need to speak with you privately." Hannah held her breath. Gaelon's tone was nothing less than threatening. "Come with me," he said, leading her out into the portal.

Hannah fought to keep her wits about her. She had dealt with blackmailers, but there was more at stake than a café. Concern for her daughter's delicate condition and the potential danger to her loved ones loomed before her. Trying to keep a clear head, she glanced to the end of the hall where Sophia nodded, smiling, as if to say, "go ahead mother, we can take our walk later." Gaelon closed the door.

Thank the Lord that there is no carriage of doom waiting to whisk me away to God only knows where, Hannah thought. *Hurry, Naomi!*

"I thought that we had an understanding," Gaelon said with a melancholy tone. When I left for Belgium, I believed that we shared a mutual trust."

Ah, he is going to use our relationship to put me off guard. The pathetic tone, too, so that I pity him. She made no reply.

"A situation has arisen that makes me question that trust, Hannah."

You need not tell me.

He then turned his back to her.

What was he doing? He was reaching into his coat! Did he have a pistol or a rope? She searched the grounds for a witness to this eminent crime. There was no one. She would have to attack first

Now! She leapt on him, grabbing him by the shoulders, knocking him to the porch floor. His head hit the steps.

"Hannah!" Rahzvon called out, and ran to them. She quickly moved from Gaelon's back. He lay there motionless.

Rahzvon knelt down, trying to revive his brother, "Gaelon! Gaelon!" He gently turned him over. Beneath him lay a small, flattened bouquet.

Hannah's eyes widened in horror. "What have I done?" she gasped. "I thought he—"

Rahzvon held Gaelon's wrist, checking for a pulse. Gaelon then groaned. "I think he is fine, except for this nasty bump on his head."

"Rahzvon, it was a mistake, I assure you," she said regretfully.

"Trust me; I know exactly how you feel. I did the very same to your brother in London. Thanks to Hiram, the law did not lock me up and throw away the key. I guess your frolicking went a bit too far," Rahzvon grinned and raised a brow.

"Yes," she mumbled.

"Not to worry. Eloise can give him an ice bag for his head. Here," he said, snagging the bouquet and the card lying from the floor. "No need to press these."

Hannah's trembling hands accepted the card. She could not bear to read it, but knew it was a deserving punishment.

For the Loveliest Lady in Lochmoor

Hannah closed her eyes with regret, and then opened to see the signature.

Your devoted servant,
Desilama

Desilama?

Gaelon groaned again. "What happened?"

"You fell, Gaelon," Rahzvon grinned sympathetically at his mother-in-law.

Hannah dropped the flowers and helped Rahzvon lift Gaelon to his feet.

"Inside," Rahzvon instructed. His brother grimaced, feeling the bump on his head and retired to the parlor divan. "I will fetch Eloise for an ice bag. If you two will excuse me, these chores left me famished."

Gaelon took Hannah's hand and confessed, "You know, I deserved that fall. I was about to make you feel guilty for my jealousy. As the good Lord would have it—not on his watch. The slate floor must have been damp from the morning dew."

Hannah listened. These were not the words of a blackmailer, or of a man, who would court her while double-crossing her brother. The final proof appeared in the form of a slip of paper that Gaelon withdrew from his pocket.

He opened it. "I, I," he grimaced with pain, "I have a poem to read to you. I did not author it, but I thought that you would like it."

Hannah's hand covered her mouth in astonishment and shame. She left the divan and stepped away. Gaelon got up, trying to straighten his battered muscles.

"Hannah, I have offended you. I do not have to read the poem. I am not deserving of your audience. Here, I shall toss it into the fireplace." He turned toward the hearth.

"No! No!" She ran to stop him.

"M' lady, beautiful lady, you are trembling. My fall frightened you. But look, I am a bit bruised, that is all." He took her hand and placed the poem in it. "I admit that I was afraid that you saw me leaving the study after getting the poem. I scanned nearly a dozen volumes, from Emerson to Yates, for the perfect verse. I truly wanted it to be a surprise—more so than Mr. Raheleka's bouquet."

Hannah held back the waves of emotion determined to drown her. She stared at the paper in her hand. No one had ever chosen a poem for her—a truly romantic gesture.

"Gaelon, I am sorry I spoiled all of this."

He opened his arms, "May I?"

Hannah moved to his slight embrace, as his pain from the fall was increasing. "I guess the fall was fate's way of making us closer," he said, placing his cheek next to hers. "Now, cheer up."

"You will have to excuse me, I am not myself. Hiram has left his bed and gone to the village. I am concerned for his health."

"The village?" Gaelon walked Hannah to sit with him on the window seat.

"Yes, the telegraph office with Livia. Urgent business, I believe."

"But Edward and I were to handle his business matters."

"You know Hiram. He is stubborn and insists upon being in charge."

"Indeed. If you will excuse me, I think that I shall lay down for a bit."

"Certainly."

He left the parlor and entered the hall. Hannah unfolded the paper and began reading:

Tomorrow we meet the same then, dearest?
May I take your hand in mine?
Mere friends are we,—well friends the merest
Keep much that I resign

For each glance of the eyes so bright and black
Though I keep with heart's endeavor,—
Your voice,

"This is a verse from Robert Browning's 'Lost Mistress'! Your intentions may have been well-meaning, Mr. Sierzik, but this is rather unappealing source," she said, folding the paper and placing it into her pocket.

The McDonnally coach had nearly reached the village business district, when Livia noted that Hiram had been surprising quiet for the last couple of miles.

"Darling, how are you feeling?" she inquired, touching his hand, noting his chalky complexion.

He turned slowly to face her.

"Livy, please, please have the coachman stop the carriage."

Livia tapped her umbrella on the ceiling. The carriage stopped. She could hear Hiram's deep breaths.

"I need some air," he said with a painful tone.

Livia slid quickly from the seat, opening the door. She climbed out and offered him a hand to steady him, as he left the coach. He straightened and took a deep breath. "I need to walk."

She took his arm. Two steps later, he stopped and leaned into the carriage and then collapsed down to the ground.

"Hiram!" She looked to the driver, "Help me!"

He jumped down and pulled a blanket from the carriage to place under Hiram's head, now drenched with perspiration.

"We have to get him to the doctor! Help me get him into the carriage!" Livia demanded.

"Mum, that would be impossible. You and I canna lift the master. I'll unhitch one of the team and ride for Dr. Lambert."

"Go quickly. I think that he is still at the Wheaton farm. Get Rahzvon." Livia wiped Hiram's face with the corner of the blanket. The coachmen galloped off down the road.

"You will be fine, love. I promise you." She got her umbrella from the coach and opened it to shade Hiram's face. She tried to remain calm, while phrases from a dozen prayers passed through her lips. "I should have stopped you from leaving."

She closed her eyes. A tiny whimpering sound opened them. She looked curiously at Hiram. She heard it again. A small dog stood beside her wagging its tail excitedly, so that its entire back half was wiggling. For a second, the comical pup offered her a moment of relief. The shorthaired white dog with black and tan spots and lopped ears barked twice at her before doing two back flips. Livia's brows rose at the little clown's performance. She tried to smile, but turned back to dab Hiram's face. "From where did you come, puppy?" She looked up, checking the landscape for its owner. The dog moved in and began licking Hiram's face.

"No, no. I can wipe it."

The dog snuggled up against Hiram's limp body. The stray lay still, offering only an occasional wrinkled brow of concern when its eyes met Livia's. During the short wait, the unexpected visitor offered her a comforting presence.

Livia left Hiram's side when the doctor's wagon was swiftly approaching behind an equestrian.

Rahzvon dismounted asking, "How is he?"

"On fire."

Edward jumped from the wagon and placed a comforting arm around Livia. "Stubborn fool." Livia turned into his chest and wept.

Dr. Lambert, thoroughly displeased and disappointed, quickly examined Hiram. "Get him into me cart, please." He returned his instruments to his bag, mumbling, "Pig-headed chap."

The little dog went unnoticed until Edward saw it jump into the cart with Hiram. "Out of there mutt! Whose dog is this?"

Livia shrugged. Edward reached to remove the

pest, when the dog began growling with objection and curled up beside Hiram.

Livia petted the dog. "He seems to feel it his duty to protect Hiram. He has been with him since the coachmen went for help. He can stay."

The women at the manor waited impatiently for the cart, as word of Hiram's relapse had them frantic with worry. The patient arrived shortly, was soon in a fresh nightshirt, and tucked into his bed. The family congregated downstairs while the doctor spent quite a long time in his examination.

Chapter XI

"Watchdog"

"And you each gentle animal
In confidence may bind,
And make them follow at your call,
If you are always kind."

—Sarah Josepha Hale

Dr. Lambert joined the family and explained, "A serious relapse. That man canna leave that bed again until I release him. No matter what, I expect all o' ye to restrain him. There is but one o' him and many of ye. He was conscious for a moment and I warned him but he'll ne'er remember. He will sleep for a bit, but when he wakes supply him wit' as much drink and food that he will take. Keep him warm. I'll be returnin' this evenin'."

Livia entered Hiram's room and took her usual post in the rocking chair next to the bed. She, too, was soon dozing, from the stress of the day. Eloise and Hannah entered the room a half hour later with fresh towels and tea for her.

"That poor woman," Hannah whispered to Eloise. "I am not certain that this naughty brother of mine deserves her."

Eloise dampened a cloth in the basin and wiped Hiram's forehead. "Very feverish." She repeated the process, and then rinsed the cloth, wrung it out. She hung it on the towel bar and walked to the foot of the bed where Hannah stared at her brother.

Eloise shook her head. "The handsomest man I have ever seen, looking his absolute worst."

A wild rippling movement beneath the covers on Hiram's right caught their attention. Both women straightened with a start and exchanged a fearful glance.

"There is something in there with the master!" Eloise whispered and grabbed a hold of Hannah's arm.

"Good grief, it is probably Rusty."

"No, Mum, he cannot jump up onto the bed. It is probably the cat."

Hannah bravely whipped back the blanket.

"Ah!" Eloise shrieked at the sight of the strange dog snarling at them.

Livia woke with a start, knocking the teacup from the table next to her. Hiram stirred only slightly.

"What is it?" Livia asked with alarm.

"Look, there is a strange dog in with Hiram." Hannah pointed to the yawning stowaway.

Livia grinned at the familiar face. "You're back." She walked over to the opposite side of the bed. "He was with us when Hiram had his spell on the road and rode back with us in the wagon and he obviously found his way in."

Hannah scowled. "It has to go! We shan't have that dirty creature in here contaminating the linens." She reached for the dog, which produced a low warning growl.

"I think I should try. He knows me," Livia said, cautiously moving toward the bed. "It is all right. We are going to bathe you. Then you may return."

"Livia, I think not," Hannah objected. "It may be rabid or something."

"Not to worry, I will keep an eye on him. He is harmless. How is Hiram?"

"Still with fever," Hannah replied.

"Could one of you please stay with Hiram? I shall be gone only for a short time."

Hannah nodded skeptically while Livia left, talking to the dog in her arms.

She carried it down to the kitchen where she met Naomi who asked, "Who is this little character?"

"Hiram's guard dog. He met us on the road when Hiram collapsed. I am about to bathe him."

"How is Hiram?"

"Still feverish, but sleeping. Hannah is with him."

"What ever inspired him to this insanity?"

"A business matter involving a missing document. That is all that I know except that had to be incredibly important. I have seen Hiram angry, but this was beyond that."

"I had better report this to Edward, so that he may investigate on Hiram's behalf. Oh, yes," she said, lowering her voice, "speaking of investigations, our detective is arriving in Lochmoor today to report his findings in Exeter."

"I nearly forgot about the mysterious Calvin Quinn. I hope it is not adverse news; this household cannot withstand much more."

"If it is bad news, we must not inform Hiram, or anyone else, as yet."

"I agree."

"I will return with the report. If Hiram wakens, give him our love. And make him behave, Livia."

"I will."

"You need not bathe the dog; Roy can do that for you. Roy!"

"Yes, ma'am?" Roy asked from the hall.

"Please take this dog and bathe it for Miss Nichols."

Roy reached for the dog. Its lip curled up and began intermittently barking and viciously growling. The servant withdrew fearfully.

Livia shrugged. "I am afraid that he is rather selective in the company that he keeps. Thank you, but I shall bathe him." She looked down at the pup. "You naughty boy, Roy is our friend."

Rahzvon appeared in the doorway. "What is all the racket?" He looked the dog over. "Oh, it's you." He reached over to pet the dog, intently eyeing the retreating servant.

"That is odd," Livia commented.

"What is?" Rahzvon cupped the dogs muzzle in his hands and rubbed its face.

"That dog is definitely opinionated. I am about to give him a bath. He is very attached to Hiram and uncomfortable in leaving him, even with me."

"Ah, *ganluch fatwel*, you have chosen a difficult subject—the master of this house," Rahzvon grinned.

"What did you call him?" Naomi asked.

"A Gisaleon word for what you would call a guardian angel."

"Say it again, please," Livia requested.

"*Ganluch fatwel.*"

"I think that would be the perfect name. He does need a proper name, if he is to reside here until he is claimed. Perhaps a shortened version would be better—Gantwel." Livia stroked the dog's ears.

Rahzvon burst out laughing.

"Why, why is that so amusing?" Livia frowned slightly.

Rahzvon got control and agreed, "*Gantwel* is fine."

"I like it. Why did you laugh?" Naomi asked.

"*Gantwel* is another Gisaleon word."

"Meaning what?" Livia's eyes narrowed.

"It refers to a rule that no man may move in and take over another man's home while he is incapacitated."

The women grinned at one another.

"Here, allow me." He reached for the dog.

"But your hands."

"They are fine," he said, displaying them.

"So they are." Livia smiled.

"I will bring him up to you when he is presentable," Rahzvon offered, lifting the dog from her arms.

"Thank you. I really want to get back to Hiram."

"Good morning, ladies," Rahzvon comforted the dog, as he carried it through the backdoor.

"Sophia is a fortunate woman, Livia," Naomi watched Rahzvon cuddling the stray.

"Yes, he will be a wonderful father."

Naomi raised a brow. "Yes...I will see you later this afternoon."

Livia wiped Hiram's forehead while he muttered in his sleep. "Nay, nay, it is signed! Where is it? I looked there!" He swung his head back and forth in frustration.

Hannah hung a clean towel on the rack. "He has been tossing and turning since you left. He is deeply troubled. There is no use in speaking to him; he cannot hear a word."

"*Yentrog garop oseu!*" Hiram shouted.

Livia gulped. "I guess it is for the best that we do not understand Gisaleon."

Gaelon poked his head in the door, "I should say not. He is definitely out of his head. Even in Gisaleon, I would have not said *that* in the presence of unknowing ladies." He looked at the tormented patient. "He is apparently quite upset. I will discuss the situation with Edward, immediately," he said, leaving.

Thirty minutes later, Rahzvon arrived carrying the freshly laundered guardian angel. Hiram yelled another objectionable Gisaleon phrase. Rahzvon winced. "At least his subconscious has the good sense to refrain from English."

The dog leapt from Rahzvon's arms on to the bed, and crept up next to Hiram. Hiram blurted out another phrase. The women watched Rahzvon's face turn a deep shade of scarlet.

"Please, forget every Gisaleon word that has scorched your sweet ears," Rahzvon pleaded.

Gantwel licked Hiram's cheek, turned around several times and snuggled next to him. Hiram's ranting ceased. All regarded him, amazed at his calmed expression.

Hannah folded her arms. "I was about to object to that mongrel's presence, but he accomplished what we could not—in less than five seconds. I am going to check on Sophia."

Rahzvon corrected her, "Gantwel is a *she* and Phia is napping. Take some time for yourself."

"Thank you, I will," Hannah replied, and slipped quietly into the hall.

Livia looked down at Hiram. "I am glad that he is relaxed. Your brother is going to speak to Edward about the problem."

Rahzvon sat down in the rocking chair. "Good. If anyone can resolve this, it is Gaelon. Now, you go to your room, I will stand watch...uh, sit."

"Thank you for everything." She leaned down, placing a kiss on Rahzvon's forehead.

"*Few clon huf yai!*" Hiram shouted.

They turned to see Hiram's foreboding glare.

Rahzvon gently pushed her away, "Go Livia, he is out of his head."

She scooted out the door and Gantwel quickly licked Hiram's face, sending him back into his peaceful state.

Rahzvon shuddered, mentally translating Hiram's last outburst, *you unfaithful wench!* "Thank you Gantwel. That was a little too close for comfort. You truly are a guardian angel—maybe mine, instead of his."

During the doctor's evening visit, Hiram's fever broke; he slept quietly through the night. He would wake on occasion, always greeted by a new face.

During Roy's early morning shift, Hiram commented, "I suspect that there is a path worn to my bedchamber with this changing of the guard."

"Yes, sir."

"Please send for Edward I need to speak with him."

"With no disrespect, sir, I was given strict orders to remain here until I was relieved of my duties."

"Roy, to whom are you speaking?"

"Why you, sir."

"And who might I be?"

"The boss, I mean, the master of this house."

"Go. Send for Edward, and make haste!"

"Yes, sir." Roy left immediately.

Hiram sat up in bed and stroked the little dog beneath the covers.

"You may come out now, Rusty."

Gantwel twirled around and peeked out. Hiram gave a slight jump at the sight of the unfamiliar face that appeared under his arm.

"Great Scott! Who are you?"

The pup, slipped out, shook, wagged its tail twice, and barked. Hiram laughed, "Well, hello to you, too."

The dog did not hesitate to place its front

paws on Hiram's right shoulder and lean in to lick his cheek.

"Friendly beast." He was petting the dog when he heard voices outside his door. "Quick!" he whispered, and lifted the covers for his new admirer to hide.

Livia entered the room followed by Eloise carrying a tray. In noting the absence of the "appointed guard", Livia did not know to be angry with Roy or pleased to see Hiram smiling. The latter emotion won out. Eloise left the bowl of broth and returned to her housework.

"Good day, my handsome love. How are you feeling today?" Livia asked.

"Quite well, thank you."

"And where is Roy?"

"Running an errand."

She took the hairbrush from the bureau, sat down next to Hiram, and began brushing back the black curls above his ears. "I have missed you."

He reached for her wrist, pulled her hand to his lips and kissed it. "You are very good to me, Livy. This has been quite an experience; I shan't forget the horrid nightmares; one of which I believe is of this world," he said regretfully.

"Oh?" Livia panicked, remembering the scene when she gave Rahzvon the innocent kiss of gratitude.

He ran the back of his hand along her cheek. "I am sorry that I worried you, Livy."

"I am fine. You know for a sick man, you are looking uncommonly handsome with that wild head of hair. It reminds me of you when we first met."

"Aye, not a lot of money for haircuts then. Ah, but then I was afraid to kiss you." He reached to her when the covers on his right began to move.

"Hiram McDonnally, who are you sheltering in there?" she teased.

"Oh, it is only...Rusty."

"Rusty?"

"Er...he was cold." Hiram had no sooner replied when Rusty appeared in the doorway and ran for the bed. With his paws up, balanced on his hind legs, he barked several times.

Livia looked to Hiram dubiously. "Rusty?"

Hiram smiled sheepishly when the suspect moved rapidly to the foot of the bed and jumped from beneath the covers to the floor. After a bit of growling and a sudden skirmish, Rusty fled the room with his tail between his legs and Gantwel returned to her post.

"I think he likes me." Hiram rubbed the dog's ears.

"*She* is Gantwel and yes she is very fond of you."

"Gantwel?" Hiram looked confused, familiar with the translation of the Gisaleon term.

"I *know*. I shortened Rahzvon's word for guardian angel. She has been with you since your collapse. She appeared when I was waiting for the coachmen when he went for help. Gantwel is determined to stay."

"I see. Now Livy, *she* may remain, but *you* must go."

"I beg your pardon."

"I need to dress."

"You are *not* leaving this bed, Hiram McDonnally. Have you not learned your lesson? Dr. Lambert—"

Before she had finished her sentence, Hiram was out of the bed, searching the wardrobe.

Livia quickly turned away. "It is all for naught, Hiram."

Hiram pulled open every drawer, rummaging through the bureau, as well. There was nothing to be found, but freshly laundered nightshirts.

"What is the meaning of this? Where is my clothing? Livy?" Then he was silent. Livia looked over her shoulder to see him with closed eyes gripping the bedpost to steady himself.

"Get back into bed." She rushed to assist him.

"Aye," he said begrudgingly, and climbed in.

She tucked the covers around him. "You see, it is too soon. Here now take this broth, before it is cold. You behave and you may go downstairs in a week or so." She handed him the tray.

"Another week!"

"There is no point in getting upset. You need to remain calm."

Hiram let out a low growl and took the tray. "Where is he? He should have been here by now," he grumbled.

"Who?"

"Edward."

"Please, stop talking and have your broth."

Hiram took one sip. "This is not food. Here, Gantwel." He placed the bowl down for the dog, which lapped it up happily.

"Hiram!"

"If I am forced to stay here, I will be served decent food." He laced his arms across his chest in a huff. "How am I to run my business from here?"

"It can wait. I am going to order another tray. You stay here and think pleasant thoughts."

Hiram rolled his eyes and brooded.

An hour later, Hiram rang for Roy.

"How may I serve you, sir?"

"Did you or did you not notify Edward to come at once?"

"He didn't show up?"

"Obviously, not."

"Something must have delayed him, sir."

"Had I my clothing, I would handle this myself."

"Is that a request, sir?"

"Aye, bring them to me."

"Of course, sir."

Several minutes later, Livia paused at Hiram's door.

"Come out of there and give me that, now! I demand it!" Hiram shouted.

Livia opened the door and found Hiram fully dressed, but wearing, only one boot. He was on his knees peering under the bed.

"Come out of there, Gantwel!"

"Hiram McDonnally, you promised," she scorned.

Hiram turned to see Livia with her hands on her hips looming over him. He stood up and looked down on her. "Livy, I have to take care of this matter. Our financial future is at extreme risk."

"Gantwel, bring it to me," she ordered.

The dog peeked out from beneath the bed, with the boot between its teeth. It crept stealthily behind Hiram and over to Livia. She reached down and took the boot. Hiram shook his head and put out his hand. Livia gave one quick pitch toward the open window. The crash that followed left the three of them wide-eyed.

Livia waited in the hall while Hiram pouted,

muttering colorful Gisaleon phrases, while he changed back into his nightshirt.

"Traitor," he mumbled at Gantwel, watching him from the bed.

Livia knocked.

"Come in," Hiram grumbled.

"Consider yourself fortunate. Had Gantwel and I not ended this expedition, you may have found yourself unconscious, lying on the grounds again. Now, how did you get those clothes?"

"Roy. I am giving him a raise in pay."

Naomi poked her head in the open door. "Good morning, Hiram, Livia. Livia may I speak with you for a minute?"

"Where in the blazes is your husband?" Hiram growled.

"Running an errand, I believe. Great Scott, what happened to the window?"

Livia rushed Naomi out. "He was trying to escape."

"Find him!" Hiram demanded.

Livia closed the door and the two women walked a few steps down the corridor.

"Did you get the investigator's report?" Livia asked anxiously.

"Yes. I came over immediately to share the results with you." Naomi presented the sealed envelope. "I felt that we should read his findings together."

"Over here." Livia motioned to the small couch across from her room. "I would suggest we go into my bedchamber, but Hiram has been attempting to escape; I need to keep watch."

"Did he really try to jump from the window?"

"No, but my poor aim sent his boot into the garden and took the closed window with it."

"I thought all of his clothing had been removed." Naomi said, handing her the envelope.

"Roy brought them to him."

"Hiram must have threatened his position."

"Probably. I think Roy is a bit leery of going up against the mighty Scot." She opened the envelope. "I hope it is not bad news, Naomi." She unfolded the pages of the detective's report and held them up for them to read.

Calvin Quinn
Born:: January 4, 1851
Died:: March 12, 1911

Residence:: 18 Bridgemoor Lane, Exeter

Survivors: Dorian Quinn (son)
  Residence:: unknown

History

Calvin Quinn, son of Thaddeus Quinn—
Founder of Quinn Metalworks.

Quinn Metalworks sold to:
Geoffrey McDonnally (1885)

Naomi and Livia stopped reading simultaneously with a look of surprise in seeing the name of Hiram's father.

Chapter XII

"Dorian?"

"For a word spoken kindly
Hath power to heal;
But a word spoken harshly
Is venomous steel."

—Clarence Gibbs

Naomi and Livia continued reading the Quinn document.

Calvin Quinn, pauper,
Places infant son, Dorian, in foundling home.

"Oh," Livia sighed. "Poor man—poor child."

"A pauper so soon after Geoffrey purchased his company?" Naomi questioned suspiciously.

"He may have been a gambler and lost all of his money."

"In a year's time? And he gave up his child?"

"There is no mention of a wife. He probably could not raise the child properly, alone," Livia suggested.

"No, there is more to this. Why would Geoffrey have the Quinn name hidden in the box, much less, on the top shelf where no one was likely to find it for centuries? In passing, the other day, I asked Edward if he knew anyone of the name Quinn."

"*Naomi.*"

"I know, I was taking a chance, but if it was a familiar name in their business dealings, there would be no point in pursuing this."

"What was his reply?"

"He had never heard of it."

"Never? But surely there was a record in Geoffrey's file of the purchase."

"Obviously, not. Edward knows the history of the McDonnally holdings like the back of his hand."

"Then why would Geoffrey keep a record of the name?"

"I am not sure. Perhaps, he had need to refer

to it at a later date."

"Or his conscience inspired him to record it with hopes that someone would find it in the future."

"Livia, you give the man too much credit. From what I have heard, he was not sentimental or benevolent in business. No, I think this requires further investigation into the purchase and the loss of Mr. Quinn's money."

"I agree."

"Let us keep these findings discreet. Hiram and Edward have enough to tend to."

Livia nodded.

"I will wire Mr. Jorgensen at once to investigate the details and retrieve more information about the son. Mr. Jorgensen makes a habit of providing information, bit-by-bit, to insure further need of his services," Naomi said, receiving the envelope from Livia.

"Thank you for bringing it. I had better get back to Hiram. Dr. Lambert will be arriving, soon."

"We will not let this rest, until we uncover the truth," Naomi announced and looked up to see Roy's pale face. He rushed toward the staircase.

"Poor Roy. He must have thought you were talking about his supplying Hiram's escape attire." Livia grinned.

Dr. Lambert arrived punctually for Hiram's appointment, and was greeted by Hiram's protective canine companion.

"Easy, lassie, I am here for a good cause," Dr. Lambert said in a soothing voice. "Hiram, I understand that ye havena been followin' me orders."

"Well, Gantwel, your self-appointed assistant,

prevented that. She stole my boot."

"Aye, I heard it made its way to yer garden. So, she is still wit' ye?"

"Livy or the dog?"

The doctor chuckled. "Do you think ye could persuade yer watchdog to let me examine ye?"

"Aye. Gantwel, get down." The dog did not move. "I said, get down!" Hiram lifted the stubborn pup to the chair next to the bed. Gantwel immediately started whimpering, staring at the wall. The two men looked curiously at her. Hiram rolled his eyes. "Good grief."

The doctor placed the stethoscope on Hiram's chest. "Take a deep breath."

"Might I ask you a question?"

"After ye take a deep breath." Hiram breathed in. "Good, verra good."

"You saw how that dog reacted when I instructed her to leave."

"Aye, a wee sensitive she is—a typical lassie."

"That is exactly my point. Every woman, to whom I speak in an elevated voice, is reduced to tears or whimpering: Livy, Naomi, Eloise, Marvel Wheaton, the dog."

"Marvel Wheaton?"

"Aye, 'tis personal, concerning Edward's stamp album."

"Ah. Now, ye stop talking and open yer mouth and say 'ah'."

"Ahh. Is it only me, or do all men share this difficulty?"

"Yer throat looks better. I am many years yer senior, Mr. McDonnally, but I hae a wife and daughters. It is their way. They hae different weapons to fight than we. They aim directly for the heart—not intentionally, mind ye. I believe it to be instinctive. It is there way o' defendin' themselves."

"What do you do in these cases?"

The doctor removed his stethoscope and placed it in his bag. "Avoid it. They are goin' to start bawlin', so avoid it."

"Do nothing, say nothing?"

"Nay. For example, when me wife does somethin' that I dunna approve, I speak in a verra controlled tone—gentle as a summer breeze. She canna cry wit' nothin' to provoke her. I dunna lose a battle out o' guilt."

"Do you ever win?"

"I didna say that, but they can ne'er make ye give in by weepin'. Try it."

Hiram squinted skeptically.

"A few more days in this bed and then ye can be out for a good half day at a time. After a week, ye should be fine, if ye slack up on yer chores. I dunna want a permanent position here."

"Aye. Could you please tell Livy to come in?"

"Aye, take care. Lots o' drink. Send for me if ye need me. Remember, rest."

"Good day and thank you, doctor."

Livia entered and Gantwel willingly hopped onto the bed, when Livia instructed her off the chair. Hiram raised a brow at the dog's compliance.

"What did the doctor say?" Livia asked.

Hiram observed her curiously.

"Hiram, is something wrong?"

"Nay, I am well...planning my strategy for recovery."

"Excellent."

"Livy, I need to get to the telegraph office."

"You are not going anywhere. A servant can deliver your message."

"Nay, I cannot do that."

"Then, I shall take it."

"Nay, Livy."

"You do not trust me?"

Control. "I never said that...Love."

"You most certainly did. You implied that you did not wish for me to send it. I thought that we were to be married and that you honored my trust over everyone."

"Livy, darling, I never said that I did not trust you." *As a summer breeze.* "It is simply something that I need to do myself." He smiled genuinely.

"Well, you cannot and you obviously do not believe me to be capable. Is that the reason?" She left the chair and began to pace.

Her voice had changed since the onset of the conversation. He detected her original rejection replaced with a melancholy disappointment. The red flags were rising. He watched her deliberate pace, which modified to an aimless meandering about the room.

"Livy, you are jumping to conclusions—not that that is wrong, but I know that you are a very intelligent, capable woman."

She turned, downcast. "It is the contents of the telegram. You do not feel that our relationship warrants me to be privy to that information."

"Livy, how dare you insinuate that I do not love you enough to confide in you? Have you no faith in me?" the inquiry shot from his lips. "I am disappointed in you, Livy," he said sharply.

That was the point of no return and Hiram knew it from her expression. His candor was fuel for the flame. She burst from the room. Her haunting sobs trailed after her down the hall. Hiram fell back to his pillow and glared up at the ceiling. Gantwel left his side and went to the door, refusing to leave, but staring down the hall.

"Gantwel, come back here!" he shouted. The dog refused to budge or look at him. "Blast it! Get back here!" The dog remained seated and began whining. "Perfect! Women!"

Hiram threw back the covers and went to the door where he found Rahzvon sitting guard, reading a book.

"Going somewhere, Hiram?" Rahzvon shook his head with an expression of disapproval.

"Nay...only checking to see what you were reading!"

Rahzvon held up Livia's novelette and grinned.

Hiram went inside and slammed the door. "Perfect!"

Hiram had no sooner returned to his bed when Hannah stormed in.

"What have you done to Livia?" She glanced down at Gantwel, still whimpering. "And what is wrong with that dog?"

"You are interfering, my *dear* sister."

"I do not care what you think. Livia is my friend and I take offense." Hannah put her hands on her hips. "I consider an attack on Livia as a personal insult toward me. The world is upside-down and I shan't tolerate a war within the clan!" She shook her finger at him, "You had better amend this Hiram." She then sped from the room, conveniently ignoring his rebuttal.

"How am I to make amends when she is out there and I am incarcerated in here?" he shouted.

Gantwel returned to her post on the chair. A moment later, Hannah nudged Livia through the door.

"Apologize to her, Hiram."

"Please sit down, Livy. Get down Gantwel!"

The dog lay down on the chair and whimpered. Livia petted her and gave Hiram a you-mean-man look.

"I was *trying* to make a chair available for you, Livy."

She picked up the brutalized animal and sat down with it on her lap. "You should get some rest, Hiram."

"How can I have any peace with every female on the estate angry with me?"

"I am not angry with you," she said softly.

"Well, that is the first bit of good news of the day."

"I am disappointed."

Hiram dropped his head in frustration. "Livy, I said that I was sorry."

"No you did not."

His head rose. "I most certainly did. I said that I trusted you."

"*That* is not an apology." She turned to face the window.

Hannah poked her head inside and seeing Livia's apparent discontentment, queried, "What? Have you not apologized?"

"*Hannah!*" Hiram reprimanded.

"Edward is here to see you!" She slammed the door closed.

Hiram turned to Livia. "Livy, I am sorry—you hear me saying it. Now, I need to speak with Edward."

She left the chair and placed the dog on it. She was leaving the room when Hiram called out, "We will talk, later!"

Edward entered after her.

"Edward, I am in the midst of a financial crisis and now, now, that!" Hiram shook his finger at the door.

"You are preaching to the choir, man. I am ashamed to admit it, but I am at loss when it comes to domestic affairs and frankly, at a loss as to what is the urgency in your financial affairs."

Hiram pointed to the top drawer of the Duncan Phyfe table beneath the window. "Open it and reach into the compartment in the back. Pull out the letter." Edward did as instructed. "Read it."

Edward looked fearfully at the envelope, opened it, and read the enclosed correspondence.

"Hiram, this cannot be! This has to be a mistake!" He dropped to the edge of the bed. "Now, I understand."

Hiram sat up straight. "You were there when I signed the contract and you were present when the courier delivered the final papers."

"I was. But this can be cleared up. You need only present them as proof of the transaction."

"Aye, if I had them! They are missing from my desk!"

"Missing? Who would have taken them? You keep the drawers locked, do you not?"

"Aye. Did you leave them unlocked?"

"I resent that remark, Hiram."

Hiram dropped back and sighed, "Maybe I am responsible. I am not certain. I was ill the following week and I cannot remember."

Edward left the bed. "Ailsa Shipbuilding should have a copy!"

"Obviously not. It is too late. You read it; they have merged with another company. I doubt they ever received our contract and someone forged the names on our returned copy, accepting our offer."

"But, we needed their contract to complete the fleet project!"

"Blast it, I know!"

"Who could be responsible?"

Hiram clenched his teeth and stared into Edward's desperate gaze. "I think I know who it is."

"Who?"

"Trust me, it is in your best interest to remain ignorant of my suspicions. I need to wire a contact. He will have the necessary information to verify the suspect."

"I can send the wire."

"Nay, you cannot. It has to be sent immediately. Is Desilama still in Lochmoor?"

"He is visiting this evening before he leaves tomorrow."

"Grand. I need him for a brief meeting. He may be our only hope."

"I will send him over as soon as he arrives. But you know, Hiram, it is too late."

"Aye, but I have connections with the Royal Navy. We will see how the tables turn." Hiram opened his hands and stretched his fingers. "I *will* say that it is pleasant to speak with someone of my gender—someone who is not twisting my words and falling to pieces every other minute."

"I shan't comment on that subject, or it shall surely come back to haunt me. The women have eyes and ears everywhere," Edward said, grinning.

That evening Desilama reported to Hiram's room. Hiram placed his supper tray on the side table.

"Thank you for coming, on such short notice,

Desilama. I apologize for disturbing your plans for the evening, but this is a matter of great urgency."

"I am honored to assist you. The McDonnallys have been a second family to me."

"If this is true, which I believe to be, you will protect Edward by not revealing anything I say tonight—not to him, nor anyone else."

"You can trust my discretion, sir."

Hiram explained the situation in depth and gave specific instructions in handling the investigation, which would confirm or discount Hiram's suspicions.

Desilama approached the door. "I shall send the wire, then contact the other two tomorrow morning."

"I thank you, Mr. Raheleka, in behalf of my family. There would be no recourse without your involvement."

"I would say that it is my pleasure, but this task could lead to a grave situation for the McDonnallys."

"Aye," Hiram said soberly.

The next day, Hiram tried to enjoy Sophia's company as they engaged in a brutal game of chess.

"Uncle Hiram, are you certain *that* is a legitimate move?" Sophia complained.

"'Tis. Checkmate. Had you read that book that Daniel gave you, you would be familiar with such strategies."

"I shall never win." She replaced the pieces to the box.

"Study and you may win the next." Hiram stretched. "Sophia, I need you to do me a favor."

"You need a bite to eat? I am on my way to

the kitchen."

"Nay. George Hicks, my accountant will be visiting this afternoon and I do not want your mother speaking to him."

"Why?"

"I do not approve of mixing business with family."

"Very well, but your worries are for naught. Mother, is not even slightly attracted to the man. She has enough to keep up with Gaelon and Mr. Raheleka."

"Please, Sophia, keep your commentaries on your mother's social life to yourself."

"Yes, sir." She kissed his forehead. "I shall do as asked."

Hiram blew out a sigh of relief and closed his eyes.

In the west wing, under Allison's instruction, the children of Livia's School of Little Dreams were practicing their numerals on the provided slates. Livia was placing new volumes on the table when Naomi appeared in the doorway.

"Livia, it has come! A wire about Mr. Jorgensen's report!" she whispered. "He has found Dorian Quinn and has news of extreme importance concerning the McDonnally purchase of the Quinn Ironworks!"

"So soon?"

"Yes, and he wants to speak with us at my home this afternoon at one-thirty."

"I am to have lunch with Hiram at twelve. I will meet you afterward," Livia said eagerly.

"Very good." They grasped hands and looked at one another anxiously.

Chapter XIII

"Adoption"

"A bad penny always comes back."

Mr. Jorgensen arrived ten minutes late, which seemed like an eternity for Naomi and Livia.

"Mrs. McDonnally, Miss Nichols, the information I am about to reveal is not only shocking, but extremely sensitive. Dorian Quinn is living here in Lochmoor Glen."

"Where? How is this possible? I know everyone in the village." Naomi asked.

"My dear ladies, he was adopted as an infant and living with another name. *He*, in fact, is not aware of his true identity. This is the truth. I have my sources."

Truly shocked and amazed by the discovery, the women could not believe it.

"Who is he?" Livia asked.

"Someone with whom you are quite well-acquainted. Prepare yourselves, ladies."

Dorian Quinn was someone they knew living in Lochmoor Glen? Livia and Naomi replied in unison, "Henry McTavish?"

"No. Mr. Guillaume Zigmann."

"Guillaume?" Naomi whispered. She swallowed hard. She turned to her wide-eyed accessory.

"Guillaume is adopted?" Livia asked with disbelief.

Mr. Jorgensen nodded. "Aye, Mum. The records were confidential, but in light of the information about the McDonnally purchase of the Quinn Ironworks, I thought that it vital that you have this information."

"Continue," Naomi mumbled.

"History has it, that the company was indeed purchased by Geoffrey McDonnally. Calvin Quinn received a fair sum, however not enough to satisfy his past debt to Mr. McDonnally. Therefore,

Geoffrey garnished nearly every wage that Mr. Quinn earned until he died two years ago. The monies were deposited into a McDonnally account entitled the 'Q Savings'."

"It is no wonder that Mr. Quinn put his son in a foundling home," Livia deduced. "Guillaume in an orphanage?"

Mr. Jorgensen continued, "The urgency in the matter relies on the fact that an unknown source has determined that the actual debt to the McDonnallys was paid in-full ten years ago. Thus, ten years of that money will be confiscated and reclaimed by Calvin Quinn's only heir, Dorian Quinn—better known as, Guillaume Zigmann."

"Great Scott!" Naomi left her chair.

"Unfortunately, Mum, Geoffrey McDonnally invested the sum of the said 'Q Savings' in any number of companies which earned significant dividends; all of which legally belong to Mr. Quinn. Now, I shall take leave of you with my discretion. However, this scandal shall not remain a secret for long; it shall become public knowledge very soon— but not of my doing, I assure you. The information is yours, as is my bill." He handed Naomi the invoice. "Good day, ladies."

Naomi and Livia stood dumbfounded, frozen in thought.

"Is it not a fateful coincident that Guillaume came to live on Geoffrey's estate?" Livia questioned.

"Coincident—not likely," Naomi said without hesitation.

George Hicks, Hiram's accountant took a chair next to Hiram's bed promptly at two o'clock.

"What is the status, George?"

"It is not good news. The audit did not go well. I have a list of the companies purchased with the dividends of the Q Savings investments. It is an exorbitant amount. Your father had monies accrued from said Calvin Quinn from the time of the purchase of the Ironworks until Quinn's death two years ago. Hiram, I am sorry to say that a substantial amount of this money was illegally appropriated. The barrister, a friend of the late Calvin Quinn, made the discovery and intends to take immediate action in recouping it, as well as compensation for damages due to the Quinn family."

"Give it to them. I am in no need of a scandal."

"Hiram, the money was illegally acquired over a ten year period."

"Ten years?" Hiram shot from his bed.

"Yes, actually, the debt was paid in full ten years ago."

"How much?" Hiram stopped pacing and asked.

"I am afraid that you will be forced to liquidate a great number of your companies to compensate the Quinn family."

Hiram rubbed his forehead anxiously, "Dear God, my father has done this to me!" Hiram moved sporadically around the room, and then stopped. "Who are they, these Quinns?"

"Not they, one man alone. One son—Dorian Quinn."

"Surely we can negotiate with the man!"

"I have no information regarding him or his whereabouts, but I am certain that this information is eminent."

Hiram grasped the drapes and stared out to

the garden where Livia's students were playing follow the leader with Guillaume.

"Hiram, with the new merger, I do not think that this shall be a problem. The fleet shall bring in a considerable profit."

Fleet! There is no proof *of the merger!* A voice screamed in his head. "Get out George. I need to be alone—to think."

Hiram had already suffered from considerable sales of his German companies, which he made in fear of the rising conflict. Now upon losing the fleet contract and the Quinn family claim, his head was spinning with thoughts of cutting his losses. He returned to his bed, with the thought that Desilama would soon be arriving with news of the suspected thief of his missing contract. He leaned back, feeling as though the entire third and fourth floors had caved in on him. He closed his eyes remembering the last time he felt this way—the day that Kade was no longer a part of his life.

I wanted to drink it all away, but Livy was there. He turned over and opened his eyes. It was not like the day at Hailes Crag when Naomi found him drunk in the bothy. *Nay I did not have Livy, then. I have her now.* "Oh, Livy, please do not judge me for my father's greed. I will make it up to you."

Gantwel, who had taken refuge beneath the bed during George Hicks memorable visit, crawled out and jumped up beside Hiram. She curled up next to him after three turns and laid her head on his shoulder.

"Forgiving soul."

He closed his eyes. Stroking his companion, he envisioned the bottle of scotch sitting on the table of the bothy.

Gantwel licked his face.

"Aye, lassie, 'tis the coward's escape. But, I am not feeling at all brave right now. I have entirely too many crucial decisions to make."

Early that week, Hiram was free to move around the mansion. His afternoon nap ended with Desilama's return to the manor.

The messenger had no sooner entered Hiram's bedchamber and closed the door, when he announced, "Hiram, good news! The pirate is not Gaelon Sierzik, as you suspected."

Hiram fell back and relaxed. "Thank you dear Lord; at least I do not have to deal with that." He sat up on the bed edge. "Then who?"

"The owner of the company who accrued the new contract with Ailsa—Hester Carlson."

Hiram lunged forward. "Hester Carlson?" He left the bed and began to pace. He stopped. "She was in this house prior to my signing the merger, but the contract had not been finalized. She could not have been the one. It was here after she left."

"Perhaps, she is not working alone, despite her denial to having an accomplice. The culprit may be under your roof, as we speak."

"Naturally," Hiram said with defeat.

Livia met Hiram in the parlor the next morning. Resigned to conceal her knowledge of Guillaume's identity, she directed the conversation to topics concerning her school. Hiram listened as attentively as possible, trying to suppress his anxiety for his financial problems and his concern that the contract thief was there living in his home.

After asking a number of Hiram's opinion's on

a variety of subjects, Livia left the divan.

"Hiram, I realize that you are preoccupied, but you have not heard a word that I have said."

"Love, I am sorry. There are so many things on my mind."

Livia was about to explode; she felt horrible about withholding the information about Guillaume and the devastation the Quinn claim was to have on Hiram's fortune. She could wait no longer; she may be holding pertinent evidence.

"Hiram, may we speak privately in your study?"

"Of course, Love." He took her hand and led her into the study. He smiled like a man anticipating a sweet diversion and closed the doors behind them. "You are looking exceptionally bonnie today, Livy." His eyes twinkled as he stepped next to her and placed his hands on her shoulders. He leaned down and they shared a kiss that seemed to never end and may not have, if Livia's conscience would not have pulled her away.

"Hiram, there is something that I need to tell you. You are not going to be at all pleased."

Hiram's arms dropped limp to his sides. "Not another man—another suitor," he said, shaking his head.

"Please remain calm, dear. I do not want you to suffer another relapse." *I have to tell him about Guillaume, first.* "It is about a man—Dorian Quinn. He—"

"Dorian Quinn?!" Hiram's black eyes ignited. He stepped back. "I knew it! No matter how complex—how devastating things had become—I knew that it would get worse!" He began pacing madly.

"Hiram, I—"

"Fate has cast the final blow! Cruelty and justice tread behind me like a relentless shadow. Everywhere I go—another turn of events, worse than the last! Any man in the universe, but nay it had to be Dorian Quinn with whom my woman is involved. Do you have any conception of the odds of this occurring? Nay, it is my life's fate!"

"But—"

"There is nothing that you can say, Miss Nichols. I wonder why I dared return to Lochmoor Glen. In Switzerland, life was simple—turning the little gears, sitting peacefully in the back of the shop, and—"

"Hiram!"

"Livy my world is falling apart! Have you no mercy!" He resumed his pacing.

"Hiram, it is Guillaume!"

With that statement, Hiram's anger increased a hundredfold. *"Zigmann?* Zigmann! Livy, how could you?" he shouted and grabbed the nearest chair, knocking it to the floor. He was out of the study before Livia could say another word. She ran to the hall where she saw him moving fast and furious toward the backdoor.

"No, Hiram, wait!"

Hiram ignored her cries. "He shall pay! How dare he cross me in my own home?"

The garden gate crashed into the fence as his stride lengthened toward the cottage where Guillaume sat playing quietly with Rusty on the porch.

"Wait Hiram! You do not understand!" Livia called, chasing after him.

Seeing Albert trimming the shrubs, Livia pleaded for his assistance, "Albert! Stop him! Stop him!"

Albert took off after Hiram, who was moving in like an ominous twister. Guillaume looked up fearfully and backed toward the door as Hiram's foot hit the first step.

"Zigmann, I am going to—"

"No, he is *Dorian Quinn!*" Livia's words screeched through the moors. Hiram stopped.

It was silent as though the world had stopped spinning and life had ended. Out of breath, Livia looked regretfully toward Albert, who lowered his head. Hiram stared at Guillaume who was cowering behind his twisted shirtfront tight in Hiram's fist. Hiram slowly released his grip and stepped back, glaring at Guillaume. "You?" Hiram muttered.

"Who? Me?" Guillaume looked perplexed toward Livia and then at his solemn father. Guillaume cleared his throat and whispered to Hiram. "Sir, I believe Miss Nichols has a problem, if you know what I mean. I am sure the stress of your illness has taken its toll on her. Surely, a bit of bed rest is all that she needs. You can see that my father, too, is concerned for her."

"What kind of fool do you think that I am, lad?" Hiram snarled.

"No, sir, I was not insinuating that you are negligent in caring for Miss Nichols! No, I was only making an observation...sir."

Livia stepped next to Albert. "I am so very sorry, Albert." A tear slipped down her cheek. She covered her mouth in shame, feeling that she had betrayed nearly everyone she loved.

Eloise stepped from the house."What goes on here? Son, what has happened?"

"Mother, do not fret. Mr. McDonnally shall handle it."

"Indeed, I shall," he said with a voice of doom. He left the porch and snagged hold of Livia's hand, nearly dragging her through the garden, the hall, and back to the study. He slammed the doors closed.

"What in the blazes is going on, Livy?"

"I am sorry. Naomi and I found out only recently.

"*Naomi?*" he questioned with contempt.

"Hiram, it is very lengthy and complicated."

"I have the time," he said bluntly, dropping to his desk chair and swiveling toward her. His black eyes pierced hers.

At the cottage, Albert joined his wife and Guillaume on the porch. "Come inside. I need to speak with both of you."

Livia's outburst left Guillaume concerned about her erratic behavior and condition. He followed his parents into the cottage.

"How ill is Miss Nichols, father?" he asked.

"Please, sit down." Albert pointed to the couch.

"Tell us, Father, is her illness—?"

Eloise cut in, "No, no! It cannot be! Not Livia!"

Agitated, Albert demanded, "Both of you stop and please listen to me. Miss Nichols is perfectly healthy, as far as I know, and no, she has not gone mad. Ellie, I need to speak with you in the bedroom. Guillaume, wait here."

These instructions left Guillaume uneasy and curious as to the secrecy in the matter.

In the bedroom, Albert took his wife's hands in his. Guillaume moved close to the door. He strained to hear his father's words.

"Eloise, the time has come."

"What do you mean?"

"We have to tell him."

"*No*, Albert. Why?" she pleaded.

"Dear, the truth is out; Livia and Hiram know and who knows how many others."

Guillaume leaned into the door. *Know what?*

"Ellie, you have always known that this day would come. You have nothing to fear—he loves you with all of his heart. You are the only mother he has ever known."

A debilitating chill ran through Guillaume's weakening body. He stepped away and grasped the back of a chair to steady him. *Mother is not my mother?* Breathing became difficult and the walls of the tiny room began closing in on him. Eloise was his stepmother? He squinted at their family portrait over the mantle. It did not make sense. He stood perfectly still when he realized that it *was* quite possible. He remembered the night before Kade's scheduled christening when he had asked her about his. Eloise had stared blankly before changing the subject. His clouded thoughts vanished upon hearing her whimpers in the bedroom.

She needs to know that it is of no consequence. I do love her as if she were my mother. He stepped to the door and opened it without hesitation to address her.

"Dear Mother, it does not matter to me, I love you. You have been the perfect mother." He embraced her and smiled up at his father. Guillaume held her close, as he spoke. "I am so very grateful that father found you. You are the dearest stepmother a child could have."

Albert's eyes narrowed fearfully. "Guillaume."

"Yes, Father?"

"Sit down...here on the bed."

Guillaume did, not at all prepared for that which was to come.

"Son, despite everything, you have blessed our world in more ways than you can imagine. However, you need to know the truth."

"I heard Father. I understand that Mother is not my natural mother."

"Guillaume, that is not all."

"Have I siblings?"

"*Guillaume,* no, that is not what I am trying to tell you!"

"What is it Father?"

"I am not your father, Guillaume."

"Not my father?" Guillaume mumbled.

"No. We adopted you when you were an infant."

Guillaume sat speechless, while his world of innocence crashed down upon him.

Hiram and Livia sat across from each other in the study. Livia offered her explanation of the situation, confirming her understanding that Guillaume was truly unaware of his identity before today. Hiram listened intently and reiterated the financial impact of the Quinn claim.

"Livy, you should have come to me on that first day that you discovered the book—er, box. But, I understand why you did not, although I do not condone your discretion." Hiram left his chair, "Blasted! My father is still torturing me. I am ashamed to share the Geoffrey name."

"Hiram, Geoffrey is a wonderful name. Do you know what it means?"

"Doomed one?"

"No. God's peace."

He then smiled genuinely. "Well, the only peace I am experiencing is the relief that Guillaume, Dorian Quinn, is not on your historic record of suitors."

Livia forced a slight smile.

Hiram left his chair and began pacing slowly as he spoke. "We have an incredibly complex arrangement here. I am certain that things are not going well in the cottage. Indeed, it is unfortunate that young Zigmann had to learn of his background in such a manner. At least, you prevented me from breaking the poor lad in half...*poor* lad? Hardly, with the money due him. Now, how am I to approach the son of my hired help? It shan't be long before he learns of his legacy." He stopped and stood before her. "Livy, there is another urgent issue at hand."

"Allison?"

"No, she is the least of my worries. I have discovered that someone in my home has stolen a vital document."

"*Hiram*, you surely do not believe that I—?"

"Livia Nichols, why do you say such silly things? Of course, I am not accusing you. I am only curious to know if you have any information on the subject. You seem to have your hands in everything else."

"I resent that comment!"

"Sorry. Well?"

"No, I have nothing to offer in that regard."

"No one comes into this house without the servants' knowledge." Hiram paused. "All right, I retract that statement, considering Avera's entry. The loss of that document has put my completion of an even more vital contract in jeopardy. I have to find the signed and dated copy to verify my acceptance. All that I know is that there is a great possibility that Hester Car—" He stopped, knowing that he left himself wide open for an "I told you so."

Livia raised a suspicious brow. "Hester Carlson, the woman who was in dire need of your *numerous* financial talents is involved in the theft?"

Hiram turned away and mumbled, "Possibly."

Livia elected to not sing her praises or bask in the light of her prediction of the mismatched merger with Miss Carlson. Instead, her silence on the matter was more effective. She said nothing about the despicable woman. "Hiram I am sorry this has happened. Is there anything that I can do?"

Hiram grinned, "You are a saint, my love. A sneak, but a saint." He embraced her. "Aye, there is something that you can do. Keep young Zigmann in good humor. I have to prepare a trip to Town."

"We are going to London?"

He took her hands, "Nay, I am going to London with Gaelon. We shall be in meetings every day and night, if need be. This needs to be resolved immediately, before I deal with Master Quinn." He put a finger under her chin. "I do promise to spend some time with you after this is cleared up." He leaned down and kissed her.

They stepped out into the hall and Hiram called to Roy, standing on the above landing, "Roy, prepare my holdall for three days in Town!"

"Yes, sir."

Hiram returned to his study as Livia was leaving for the west wing. A visitor rapped on the door. The housekeeper dusting in the parlor ran to answer it.

"Come in, Miss O'Connor."

"Thank you. Oh, Livia! I have a message from Mother."

Livia turned and greeted her, "Good morning." She took the folded note. "Thank you, Allison."

"Well, I need to beetle off. Guillaume is waiting for me."

"Good morning ladies," Hannah said, entering the hall from the dining room. "Is Hiram in his study?"

"Yes," Livia confirmed, stepping aside with Allison while Hannah knocked and disappeared behind the closed doors.

"Allison, Guillaume is not having the best of days," Livia warned.

"Is he ill?"

"No, but his family is going through a difficult time. I have said enough. You should not be offended if he is not in good humor."

"Thank you. Well, with Guillaume, it could be any number of things," Allison giggled and continued toward the backdoor.

"Oh, Allison, this is no laughing matter," Livia mumbled to herself.

Hannah spoke freely with her brother, "I have something that I need to discuss with you, Hiram."

"If it involves, Livy, forget it and rest assured that I apologized—countless times, and shall continue to do so for the rest of my life. Indeed, very soon, I shall demonstrate my true appreciation for Miss Livia Nichols. I have a surprise for her. Thank God it is paid in full."

"I am glad to hear it and no, it does not concern Livia. I have been withholding information from you."

Hiram lowered the stack of envelopes to his desk and listened curiously to his sister's confession.

"I should have notified you earlier, but you were ill. While you were convalescing upstairs, I came in here and noticed that the bottom drawer of the desk was unlocked."

Hiram's brows furrowed. "Why were you in my desk?"

"I saw someone leave the study—someone who was sneaking from this room."

"Who?"

"It was Gaelon. But before you jump to any conclusions, he *did* explain that he had been looking for poetry...for me."

"Poetry? In my desk?"

Chapter XIV

"Mercy"

"How sharper than a serpent's tooth
it is to have a thankless child."

—William Shakespeare

Hannah explained, "No, Gaelon actually showed me the Browning's verse that he had copied from one of the volumes. Hiram, his visit is not what concerns me."

"Then what?"

"I immediately thought Gaelon to be suspect of invading your privacy and for this, I feel ashamed. But imagining the worst, I checked to see if the desk drawers were locked, knowing that you and Edward are the only ones with keys. That is when I discovered that the bottom drawer was open. Then I saw a large form, probably that of a man, peering at me through the door crack. He quickly disappeared when I noticed him."

"Gaelon?"

"No. Eloise verified that he was in the kitchen at the time. I am not sure who it was. There are several males in the house, as you know," she said anxiously."

"Hmm." Hiram stroked his beard.

"I understand that Gaelon is accompanying you to London."

"Aye. Please look after Livy while I am away. I am feeling terribly negligent, but I have no other choice." Gantwel stood up and scratched at Hiram's leg. "This lass will need some attention, as well."

"I will keep Livia busy, but Rahzvon will have to deal with *it*." She glared down at the dog.

"Perhaps, you may not have time available?" Hiram half-smiled.

"What are you alluding to, Hiram?"

"A certain mutual friend, who seems to be quite interested in my lovely twin," Hiram suggested in reference to Mr. Raheleka.

Hannah walked to the door. "As you said,

mutual *friend*. God speed, Brother."
Hiram smiled and returned to his work.

Livia sat in her room reading the letter from Naomi:

Dearest Livia,

I hired Mr. Jorgensen to investigate the circumstances of Guillaume's adoption, intrigued by the fact that he ended up living on Geoffrey's estate. I learned quickly that for a handsome sum, this information was readily available. The sly man was withholding it, in hopes that we would request it. I succumbed to his scheme and paid.

Here is the truth according to Mr. Jorgensen. I should hope that you are seated. My desire to relay this information personally was dashed when Edward asked me to spend the day with him.

Guillaume (Dorian) was taken from the Exeter foundling home one month after he had been admitted. He was taken to Germany and placed in the care of an "unknown" couple.

Mr. J probably has this information for a bonnie price, as well.

There, the Zigmanns adopted him. Of course, they did not come to work at McDonnally Manor until years later at Edward's request.

At this point, you are surely questioning if Edward was involved in the Zigmanns and Guillaume's arrival in Lochmoor Glen. This is yet to be determined. I am in a quandary as to whether or not I should speak to Edward or contact Mr. J again. I am feeling incredibly uncomfortable with this information. I shall keep you informed as to my decision.

Love, Naomi

***

The next three days were unsettling for the McDonnally household and staff. The day after Hiram and Gaelon's departure to London, Guillaume moved into the inn where he was presented papers identifying him as Dorian Quinn. That very day, he left Lochmoor Glen. His destination was unknown to everyone, including Albert, Eloise, and his beloved Allison. His absence sent Eloise to her bed and Allison into a deteriorating state of anger and disappointment, manifesting the inevitable heartache. Albert continued with his chores, dealing with the situation in the only manner he knew—silence combined with hard work. Livia and Hannah grew closer, as the Zigmanns were withdrawn. Hannah hired a cook and another housekeeper to replace, temporarily, the devastated Eloise.

Upon hearing the news of Guillaume's departure, Tavy visited Brachney Hall to console Allison.

"Hello, Tavy," Allison greeted sullenly, when he entered the drawing room.

"Allison."

"Come, have a seat."

"Guillaume will be returnin'. Ye canna believe otherwise."

"His decisions are no longer of my concern."

"Ye canna mean that. Ye canna expect him to behave rationally after receivin' that information. He will be needin' time to sort through it."

"He acted heartlessly and irresponsibly. He left with no consideration to the couple who devoted their lives to being his parents. That is unconscionable. I am adopted and I would never put my mother, Naomi, and Edward through this. As for me, he obviously has no regard for our relationship. Did he turn to me for support and consolation? No. Guillaume Zigmann, or whoever he is, has no concept of love in any form!"

"'Tis not true Allison. In Kosdrev, when we were leavin' him guardin' the shack, his only concern was for ye and his dog. He made Rahzvon and me promise to tell ye that he loved ye and was plannin' to marry ye."

"That was a safe bet. People often say things out of guilt when they believe they are going to die."

"Nay, he said he had a ring for ye."

Her mood tempered. "A ring...for me?"

"Aye and he wanted to make certain that ye walk Rusty."

Allison's gaze fell to the little dachshund sulking at her feet. "That is all very fine, but he was not killed or captured and never presented this alleged ring. Instead, he left all of us, without a word. For that, I shall never forgive him." She looked away.

Tavy stood up. "Never is a verra long time, lassie. Think it o'er. I shall be goin', now." He turned to leave, and then turned back to her. "Allison, after me mother was killed, me father left me for two months. I needed him desperately. But, after he pulled himself together, he returned and I forgave him. It was not that he didna love me—he ne'er stopped. Guillaume loves ye."

"Good day, Tavy," Allison said coldly.

Guillaume kept his horse at an even pace on a back road heading south. He continued for miles across the moors, unaware of the landscape, lost in thoughts of his newly acquired identity. He paused at a crossroads when he saw a figure seated on a boulder in the distance. He urged the horse to move on slowly toward her. Guillaume stopped next to the woman of about his age.

"Good afternoon." Seeing no sign of any farms in close proximity, he asked. "Might I ask, what are you doing out here, alone?"

"Do not get any ideas, sir. I can take care of myself," she said tersely and climbed down.

"No, Miss, I was only concerned for your welfare."

"Well, you need not be. Heading south, sir?"

"Yes."

Noting her disheveled appearance with her patched apparel and leather satchel, he inquired, "Have you lost your horse?"

"Never had one. These feet take me anywhere that I desire."

"You mean to say that you walk *everywhere*?"

"Indeed I have—for the last four months and I shall continue to do so."

"I am impressed with your stamina."

"Would you care to sit with me for a minute?"

"I have no pressing engagements," Guillaume said, dismounting.

She offered her hand. "My name is Mercy."

He took her rather dirty hand and kissed it. "My pleasure, Mercy."

She looked at him with astonishment. "I did not expect you to...my hands are—" She quickly wiped them on her skirt. "And your name, sir? I can only imagine—being the gentleman that you are."

Guillaume looked away disturbed by the inquiry. *Guillaume or Dorian? Who am I?*

"You surely have a name—I did share mine with you." Mercy smiled at Guillaume.

He thought back to the woods at Kosdrev when he was "Robin", but today even that name linked him to his unsettling past. Instead, he chose Rahzvon's fictitious name. "Marcus."

"I like that. Marcus and Mercy. Come share my stone."

She climbed back on top of the boulder and he climbed up beside her.

"Mercy is an unusual name," he said, curiously.

"Care to hear the story behind it?"

"Yes."

"When I arrived in this world, I was a good-sized infant—not difficult to imagine seeing me, now. I have never been described as slender," she giggled.

Guillaume grinned at the stocky woman, whose round face beamed as she smiled.

"The attending nurse, surprised at my size, handed me to my mother and said, "Have Mercy!"

"My mother replied, 'I shall and I shall love her forever.' Brief, but true."

"That is a beautiful story," he said, admiring her brilliant green eyes that were fixed on his.

"Yes, but my mother's 'forever' only lasted two days. There were problems and...I never knew her."

He looked at her with great sympathy until a rush of guilt brought the memory of Eloise crying and begging him to stay. Mercy watched his expression transform to one of deep sadness.

"Pardon me." He left the rock and walked out to the field behind them. He quickly turned at the crack and the sound of pounding hooves. "Hey, come back! That is *my* horse!"

He chased after her, but the thief galloped off and disappeared behind the bend. Too exhausted to be angry, he trudged back to the rock and leaned back.

"I deserved that—the bumbling idiot, again." He kicked the dirt.

A minute later, he heard the slight thunder of hooves in the distance. The vagabond woman had returned. She halted next to him, but did not speak. Guillaume offered her a hand to climb down.

"You probably thought that I was stealing this fine animal." She ignored his offer and patted the horse's neck.

"No, I would never think that," he lowered his hand and grinned.

"It has been such a long time since I had the pleasure to ride such a beauty."

"How was it?"

"Excellent."

He offered her his hand to dismount, again. She pulled her foot from the stirrup and reached for his hand. "Come on up, Marcus. This is a powerful steed. It can handle the two of us. There is a farm only a short way from here. Maybe, if we hurry, we can get in a few chores, and they will offer us supper."

Guillaume put his left foot in the stirrup and climbed up behind her.

"Hang on, Marcus!"

Their laughter could be heard at every turn as they shot toward the prospective farm.

That evening, Guillaume and Mercy stacked a chord of wood, fed a small herd of a dozen or so cows, and mucked the stalls. Afterwards they shared a meal of pork and potatoes on the back step before retiring to the barn. Guillaume spread his blanket on the barn floor while Mercy prepared her bed in the loft.

"Goodnight, Mercy!"

"Marcus?"

"Yes?"

She leaned over the edge of the loft. "I *was* going to steal your horse."

"I know, Mercy. What changed your mind?"

"Your expression when I mentioned my mother. Do you have a mother?"

He did not know how to answer. He thought for a minute. "She is not my natural mother."

"Your stepmother?"

"No...I...was adopted." It was the first time that he had spoken the words—the absolute truth. The heartbreaking disappointment rested heavily on his chest when Mercy spoke in a melancholy tone, "I wish that I had been adopted."

His self-pity dissolved instantly; he realized at that very second that he was one of the fortunate foundlings who had strangers love him enough to take him into their home and raise him as their own. Albert and Eloise had given him more than any child deserved. They *were* the perfect parents. He sat up with a start.

"Mercy—I left them—I broke their hearts—I have to go back!" He jumped to his feet and began rolling up his blanket.

She watched him tack up his horse. "Yes, you do," she sadly agreed.

"Now, you take care of yourself," he said, tying on the bedroll. "If you ever visit Lochmoor Glen, come see me." He hurriedly walked from the barn, mounted up, and trotted off.

Mercy climbed down the ladder and carried the lantern up to the loft. She turned down the flame and crawled back beneath her blanket staring at the couple of twinkling stars visible in the hole in the roof above her. For the first time in four months, she shared an evening with a friend and now he was gone. She rolled over and started to cry.

Her sobbing was cut short by the returning sound of hooves outside the barn.

"Mercy, are you awake?"

She wiped her eyes with the corner of the blanket, sat up and turned up the lantern. "Yes, Marcus. Did you forget something?" she sniffled, peering down at him.

He climbed up and stood on the ladder seemingly studying her sad expression. "I have made enough mistakes. I am a wealthy man. How would you like to live in a nice home?"

"What are you asking?"

"Can you cook?"

"Somewhat."

"My mother can teach you. I can request a position for you at McDonnally Manor."

McDonnally Manor? She was shocked.

"I know Hiram McDonnally personally. Get dressed and come with me. A beautiful woman such as yourself should not have to stack wood and muck stalls for her supper."

Beautiful woman? Only one other man had said those words to her. "I'll hurry, Marcus!"

Guillaume climbed down. "I will be waiting," he reassured, smiling like the millionaire that he was.

When the McDonnally carriage arrived,

Sophia shouted, "Uncle Hiram is back!" She ran to the hall. "Mama, Livia, Uncle has returned!"

Livia appeared at the top of the stairs. She flew down them with Gantwel at her heels. She pulled open the door to Hiram's loving arms.

"Livy, my love, how I have missed you."

Sophia stood in the archway witnessing the intimate moment between them. She noted that the kiss was no less romantic than those, which she shared with Rahzvon. Hiram's hand fell from Livia's waist to Gantwel's head, and he then looked over Livia's shoulder.

"Hello Sophia. How are you feeling?" he asked with a subdued grin.

Sophia went to hug him. "Very well, thank you. Gantwel has missed you, too."

"Aye." Hiram kissed her cheek and squatted down to play with his ecstatic companion.

Sophia peered through the open door. "Where is Gaelon?" she asked, as Hannah arrived from the kitchen.

Hiram stood up. "He did not return with me." He looked uncomfortably toward his sister. "Hello, Hannah."

With a troubled expression, she embraced him. "I am sorry to welcome you with unfortunate news, Brother."

Hiram said nothing.

"After taking residence at the inn, Guillaume left the village without a word to anyone. He had received the papers," Hannah explained.

Hiram closed his eyes and lowered his head. He let out sigh of disappointment. "And Eloise and Albert?"

Hannah reported their devastated conditions and her need to hire a cook. Sophia noted that

Allison, too, was resentful.

"These are unusual circumstances." Hiram pulled Livia next to him and rubbed the small of her back. "Love, I need to speak with Rahzvon. Sophia, where might I find him?"

"He and Tavy have gone to find Guillaume."

"Grand," he muttered.

Hannah stared at the empty carriage.

Sophia and Allison were sitting in the garden when Tavy and Rahzvon arrived. Sophia left her chair when she saw her husband walking his horse through the pasture gate.

"Rahzie, Rahzie!"

Allison watched his face light up when he handed the reins to Tavy and sprinted toward the garden gate. Allison envied every moment while Rahzvon smothered Sophia with kisses between telling her how desperately he had missed her.

Allison could not bear the pangs of jealousy; she left the garden and entered the house. She found Eloise back to work in the kitchen, peeling potatoes.

"They are back and he is not with them," Eloise mumbled.

"Yes." Allison walked to the window. Sophia and Rahzvon were still caught up in their romantic reunion. Rahzvon leaned down and kissed Sophia's belly.

"She does not know how fortunate she is," Allison muttered, returning to the table.

"He is not coming back," Eloise said wiping her eyes with her apron, and then continued peeling.

"Even if he does, I am sorry to say, but I shan't forgive him for what he has done to all of us. I never thought it possible for Guillaume to be so inconsiderate. But, then again, he is not Guillaume."

Eloise frowned to the remark.

Allison left the kitchen and continued down the hall. In passing the parlor, she saw Hiram and Livia cuddling on the divan. Allison stopped by the door before exiting.

"Now Livy, it is a surprise. No hints."

"One Hiram, one teeny, tiny one," Livia begged.

"Nay, not even a wee one."

Feeling deserted and very much alone, Allison fled to her awaiting carriage. *I cannot bear to see Mother and Edward together.* "Driver, take me to Langford," she instructed the coachmen who helped her into the carriage. Bitter, she stared stoically out the window when the Wheaton farm came into view. She shrank back at the sight of Bruce and Maryanne dancing on their porch while their children watched. She closed her eyes to escape the romance that everyone seemed to be enjoying, except her.

Several minutes passed before the driver halted the team. Allison leaned out to see what was causing the delay. A rush of sheer joy came over her. He had returned. Her heart then skipped a beat—he had not come alone.

Guillaume and the woman dismounted. He ran to the carriage.

"Allison, Love, I am back!" He reached for the door, but was not met with mutual joy.

"Allison?" He climbed in beside her. He reached for her hand.

"Do not touch me!"

"Please, please forgive me. I was a fool, but

Mercy—the girl—" he looked out where she waited, "she helped me to understand."

Allison glared at the woman donning questionable attire. "Who is she?"

"She is the guardian angel who sent me back to you and my family."

"Where did you find her?" she asked sharply.

Guillaume dropped back to the seat. "Does it matter?" he asked, annoyed by her tone.

"She looks as though she is a gypsy from the streets."

Guillaume glanced at Mercy, who offered a sweet smile. "She is. She is an orphan as I was and you were," he said pointedly. He climbed out of the carriage. "If you care to speak with me later, I shall be at home. And Allison, I have offered her a position at the estate to assist Mother. She *will* be staying."

Allison watched him climb back on his horse and help the rag-tag woman up behind him. They rode off together in the direction of McDonnally Manor.

"Take me back to the manor!" Allison shouted at the driver. *Guillaume has changed. He seems stronger and determined. Why?* She wondered if the "friend" had influenced him, as he claimed, or if knowledge of his wealth and position were responsible. Perhaps he was becoming intolerably arrogant; as he was at the time, she and he were working on constructing a kite for the contest. *Kites?* Even that had changed with the passing of the DORA act, illegalizing kite flying as a precautionary war measure. Everything had changed.

***

Eloise stood on the stool placing the freshly washed jars on the pantry shelf.

"Let me help you, Mother."

"Mercy me!" She nearly fell from the stool into her son's arms.

"That is right, Mother—meet Mercy."

The tattered guest stepped into the doorway, watching the tender moment unfold until the dashing young Rahzvon stepped next to her. Her heart nearly exploded when he spoke to her.

"Hello, Miss."

She could only nod.

Guillaume turned to the familiar voice. "Zigmann we have been combing the moors, in search of your pitiful body!" Rahzvon exclaimed, noting that the woman was attentively watching his every move. "Glad you are back."

"Yes, me too." He grinned with his arm tight around Eloise's shoulders.

Sophia moved in from behind Rahzvon. "Three of my favorite men returning in one day! Hello, Guillaume!" She ran to hug him.

Guillaume? Mercy questioned.

"How dare you worry me to death in my delicate condition?" Sophia said pitifully while rubbing her belly and glaring with disapproval at the woman still eying her husband. She left Guillaume to scoot beneath her husband's arm.

"I am sorry Sophie, Mother, everyone—I was out of my head, but—"

Allison appeared behind Sophia.

Guillaume continued, "But, I know now, how I shall handle this unpredicted chain of events." He stepped next to Mercy. "First, may I introduce, Mercy, my newest and very dear friend. If all goes well, as I expect, we shall enjoy the pleasure of her company for quite some time to come."

All looked skeptically except Rahzvon, who offered a warm welcome. Allison and Sophia were much more reserved.

"Come with me, Mercy," Eloise prompted. "I have something that I would like to give you for my gratitude."

After the two left for the cottage, Guillaume apologized to Rahzvon and Sophia, "With all sincerity, I am truly sorry for separating you two, with the baby and all. I will compensate you for your sacrifice; I am a rich man, now."

Allison smoothed her hair and looked away.

"Zigmann, you are going to have your fortune gone before you receive it!" Rahzvon laughed. "You do need to thank McTavish, too; he and I searched together."

"I shall. Now, I need to find my father. Sophia, please tell your Uncle Hiram that I am back and need to speak with him. I am certain, that he wants to speak with me."

Sophia caught Guillaume's arm. "I will directly, but first—where did you find her?"

Chapter XV

"The Perfect Presents"

"Surely goodness and mercy
shall follow me all the days of our life."

—Holy Bible

"Travelling alone, like myself. Except on foot." Guillaume explained to Sophia about his first encounter with Mercy. He then left through the back door.

Allison remained silent. Sophia was not satisfied with his brief account, but addressed Rahzvon, "Darling, Uncle wants to speak with you. He is in his study. Can you tell him that Guillaume wishes to meet with him?"

Rahzvon nodded and left, passing the servants, Miles and Aubrey. They were escorting Roy to the main door where the constable waited, tapping his nightstick on his palm. Roy was showing symptoms of sheer duress. Rahzvon paused with confusion of the unexpected sight and entered the study, as the doors were parted.

"Welcome back, Mr. Sierzik. Any news of Zigmann?" Hiram addressed him.

"Yes, he has returned, but on his own. He wants to speak with you."

"Good. Please have a seat, Rahzvon."

He looked around and took a seat in Livia's "reading nook." "Phia tells me that Gaelon did not return with you. Have you any word from him and...Roy, what—?"

"Aye...I will explain." Hiram sat down across from him. "Rahzvon, we have shared our differences, but I would never choose to be in this position. I will get to the point, I regret to inform you that your brother has participated in some unscrupulous and, frankly, illegal business dealings."

Rahzvon left his chair. "Gaelon?"

"Aye. This information was revealed when I discovered that I had become one of his targeted victims."

"Hefo prisehi!"

Hiram looked away. "I know that you were hoping to restore the relationship with him and—"

"Where is he?" Rahzvon demanded.

"Incarcerated. I am sorry. My charges were the first of a series of many others. I would not have believed it, but apparently his rapid path to success was anything but honorable."

Rahzvon walked aimlessly for a few steps rubbing his forehead anxiously. "Hiram, I gave him nearly all of my inheritance to invest! What is to become of his holdings?"

"Sorry—sold, split-up, to compensate as many of those he wronged, as possible." Hiram could see the desperation, fear, and shame in Rahzvon's eyes. "Lad, his offense toward me, was not stolen capital, but a signed contact, stolen with Roy's assistance. It has been recovered and dated such that my purchase of the contract is guaranteed."

"Roy, too? What will Livia think?"

"Aye, he and the conniving Miss Carlson, who had a great deal to gain from intercepting that contract. Rahzvon, Gaelon had an intimate connection with Hester. They have been working together for some time...behind her father's back."

Rahzvon grimaced and closed his eyes.

Hiram walked behind his desk.

"Rahzvon, I can prove that although you share your brother's name and were in business with him—you were not involved in these wrongdoings."

"But what about my money, Phia's, the baby's and mine?"

"This is an extremely complex case. Your brother has been involved in this treachery for years. We would desire it to be handled expeditiously, but your brother has hired a very savvy firm to represent him. It could be months, possibly years before it is all sorted out."

Rahzvon, now, breathing hard snagged a hold of the nearest chair. Hiram, a veteran of retaliation, quickly grabbed Rahzvon's forearm.

"I understand how you feel...my father...well, not here, lad—go to the barn, but first rest assured that I will do all that I can to help you recover your inheritance. You have my word."

Rahzvon stared blankly and then left for the barn.

Guillaume paused in the hall when Rahzvon blew past him, livid with rage. He took a breath and continued to the study where he found Hiram sitting at his desk with his head resting in his hands.

"Excuse me, sir?"

Hiram looked up and started to stand.

"No, please, stay seated. Is this not a good time to speak with you, sir?"

"Come on in. Please sit down. Would you prefer *Dorian?*"

"No, sir. Guillaume Zigmann is my name."

Hiram gave an approving nod.

Guillaume sat up tall. "Sir, I have a proposal—in light of my new status."

Hiram sat back.

"As you know, I am an architect and not at all well versed in the art of business affairs. I have a great deal of respect for you, Mr. McDonnally, despite the fact that your father wronged my natural father."

"Thank you, Guillaume."

"You have always treated my family with great respect and extreme generosity...and not out of compensatory guilt."

Hiram raised a brow.

Guillaume continued, "Yes, I could relieve them from your employ and build them a fabulous home, but they are quite happy with the cottage and their positions here. They would not be comfortable socializing with the upper class, nor would they be content to sit idle." Guillaume leaned toward the desk. "I need your confidence in this proposal."

"You have my discretion."

"I have accepted an offer to work at an architectural firm in London. I would like to continue with that plan."

"What do you want from me?"

"I would like to send my parents on a fortnight holiday once every six months to their chosen destination. I want you to insure that their present positions would remain secure. However, until the world affairs settle down, that may be awhile before they can actually travel."

"I can certainly honor that request. I am very pleased with their performance and friendship. Few couples could tolerate my disruptions, or should I say *eruptions.*"

Guillaume smiled. "There is one other request. The money due to me as Calvin Quinn's heir—I want it. I want it invested in the McDonnally ventures—both Edward's and yours. I trust both of you implicitly."

Hiram stroked his beard, staring at Guillaume. "Zigmann, you are a remarkable young man."

"No, sir. I was an idiot—hurting my family and friends. Oh yes, there is one more thing that I insist upon."

"Aye?" Hiram cocked his head curiously.

"Actually two. I brought back a woman. She is responsible for my return."

Again, Hiram raised a brow.

"I would like that she learn to cook under my mother's supervision. She can take over when my parents are on holiday. She is a hard worker and a decent woman."

"Very well. I trust your judgment. What is the second request?"

"I want Rahzvon and Tavy given this." He handed Hiram two slips of paper.

Hiram unfolded them and read the generous figures.

"If it is available. I gave a bit more to Rahzvon, with the baby coming."

"You *are* a remarkable man. You do the Zigmann and Quinn family names proud. I am honored to do business with you."

"Thank you, sir. Likewise."

"Quickly, go to the barn. Tell Rahzvon of your generous gift. At first he may refuse it, but it may be the answer to his unsaid prayers."

Curious, Guillaume paused, nodded and left.

The barn air was clouded with dust and Gisaleon words spoken with a great deal of anger and frustration. Guillaume stood in the doorway watching Rahzvon kicking a bale about the floor.

"Rahzvon!" Guillaume called.

Drenched in sweat and covered in dirt and bits of hay, Rahzvon stopped.

"I have good news!"

"What is it Zigmann?" Rahzvon replied, dropping to the bale.

Guillaume sat cross-legged on the floor beside

him. "Because, I am extremely grateful to you and Tavy, I have arranged for a considerable sum as a token of my appreciation to be delivered to you as quickly as possible. I will not accept any refusal—I choose to share my good fortune."

Rahzvon's gaze left the floor to the face of his unexpected benefactor.

"Rahzvon, I am not telling you this to seek gratitude, but to sincerely offer mine."

Rahzvon put his hands on Guillaume's shoulders. "I do not know what to say. It is not necessary, but is greatly appreciated far more than you can imagine. My brother is in prison and my inheritance confiscated. I shan't have access to it for a very long time, if ever. If I weren't married and soon to be—"

"Gaelon, a scoundrel?"

"Worse."

"You need not explain; I understand."

"Zigmann, we have our battles, but you and McTavish have been my true brothers. I am grateful for your friendship."

Guillaume looked to the stalls and then wiped his eyes with his cuff. "You two are my only siblings, too," he sniffled.

"Marcus!" Both men turned to Mercy's call. "Sorry, *Guillaume*," Mercy corrected.

Rahzvon grinned curiously at the friend who had borrowed his fictitious name.

Mercy continued, "You two are wanted for dinner. It will be served in a quarter hour and Mrs. Zigmann says that you had better not come until you have visited the washbasin. She says that Mr. McDonnally desires that we all dine together."

Rahzvon offered Guillaume a hand to stand and patted him on the back. "Marcus, eh?"

"I gave up *Robin,* I am moving up," Guillaume laughed.

The two men brushed themselves off when they saw an unexpected, incredible sight moving toward the barn.

"Incredible," Rahzvon commented.

"I wish it were mine," Guillaume sighed.

Allison and Mercy's absence from the dinner table was inexplicable and of deep concern for Guillaume. He had hoped that Allison would befriend Mercy, but she gave little indication in accepting her. Before his fears had peaked, the two tardy women appeared at the threshold of the dining room. Guillaume was the first to leave his seat. His instinctive response poured forth, "Mercy, you are—you are beautiful!"

"Thank you Mar—Guillaume. Your mother gave me this dress and Allison is responsible for my hair." She smiled appreciatively at the two women. Sophia squinted suspiciously.

Allison pulled out a chair, "Please, sit by me."

The men resumed their places. Guillaume was thrilled at the amicable relationship between the two women in his life. Sophia, on the other hand, was not pleased at her husband's interest with the transformation. She gave him a sharp nudge and whispered, "It is not polite to gawk."

"I am not gawking. It is amazing. Who would believe it to be the same woman?" he whispered.

"Believe it. Now, if you could take a minute for your starving wife and child, you might pass the neeps."

Hiram wiped his mouth, "Welcome, Mercy. You do look very bonnie. Now, might I ask where are your roots?"

"I have been uprooted for quite some time. I am originally from Selby, south of York, east of Leeds.

"Aye, I am familiar with the area."

Miles entered. "Sir, begging your pardon, Henry McTavish is here to see Mr. Zigmann—Guillaume."

Mercy's eyes darted to the doorway.

"Ask him in and have another place set for him," Hiram instructed.

Tavy entered smiling, delighted to see Guillaume safe at home. "Good even' everyone. I dunna want to disturb yer meal."

"Nonsense, a place is being set for you. Join us," Hiram insisted.

"Zigmann, Welcome back skinny bones!"

"Good to see you, Tavy. I have something for you."

"Aye?" Tavy turned to see the familiar feminine face. His brows met.

Guillaume began, "First, Tavy, may I have the honor of presenting—"

"What are you doing here?" Tavy nearly yelled.

Hiram laid down his fork, confused by the outburst. Guillaume glanced at Mercy, then at Tavy.

"She is—" Guillaume began.

Tavy cut him off. "I told you not to follow me!"

Mercy left her chair, raging, "I did not follow you here, Henry McTavish! How was I to know that you were here?"

All, shocked by the banter, listened with growing interest.

"You always know where to find me!" he charged.

Mercy approached Tavy, just as Trina entered

with Miles.

Mercy slapped her hands against Tavy's broad chest. "You arrogant, self-centered—" Boiling, she left the room.

Hiram broke the dead silence, "Mr. McTavish, in the future, I shan't tolerate anyone utilizing my dining room as a forum to air their differences. Now, may we continue with our meal?"

Sophia rolled her eyes at the irony of his statement.

Tavy followed Miles to his seat. "Beggin' yer pardon, sir. I was a wee taken aback by Miss Stockdale's presence.

Hiram dropped his fork to his plate. "Miss *Stockdale?*"

"Aye, I should be goin'. Excuse me."

Tavy left the room while Trina, still standing unnoticed in the commotion, slipped from the corner of the room feeling rejected, embarrassed, and miffed. She exited the mansion, by way of the nearest back exit.

Livia kept a keen eye on Hiram who was staring blankly. Her private thoughts soon became the subject of Sophia's broadcast, "Uncle Hiram, who are the Stockdales?"

Hannah, seeing Hiram's notably disturbed countenance, immediately sought to remind her daughter not to interfere. However, Rahzvon took the initiative.

"Phia, tell your mother about our engagement tomorrow morning."

Sophia's face brightened. "I thought that we were waiting?"

"No, I think that the time is right," Rahzvon insisted.

"Well, Mother, everyone, tomorrow morning

we are scheduled to visit with the current owner of what might very well become our new home! It is not too large, but adequate."

"If it all works out," Rahzvon clarified.

Hiram gave a nod of approval and discreetly dropped a bite of banger to the floor for his trusty canine companion.

Tavy left through the front door. He found Mercy standing in the drive wrapped in her tattered shawl. He stepped in front of her.

"Mercy, ye hafta leave Lochmoor Glen—this is me home. I dunna want yer father comin' here causin' trouble wit' me and me friends."

"He believes that I am in Ireland. I had a friend post a letter there from me."

"Why hae ye come, Mercy?"

"I want to live my life—make my own choices."

"Yer playin' wit' fire, in me territory. Ye'r leavin' tomorrow."

"No. I am staying." She looked sadly into his eyes. "I have missed you, Tavy."

"Lassie, it canna be. Yer father despises me." He started to reach for her then stopped. "We hae discussed this a hundred times. Only friends, Mercy, we were only friends."

"That is not what I want and I know that is not what you want either!" she called to him as he walked briskly away.

She ran and caught his sleeve. "Tavy, please!"

"It canna be! Go home to yer family!" he shouted angrily. He set out down the road to the Dugan cottage.

While the meal at McDonnally Manor was disrupted, Edward and Naomi were dining at

Brachney Hall with Beatrice and Daniel. Word that Guillaume had returned was the topic of conversation. However, Naomi was preoccupied with the unsolved mystery of the Zigmanns' employment at Hiram's home.

"To think all this time, Dorian Quinn was living on Hiram's estate," Naomi commented and looked to Edward.

"Stranger things have happened, darling— Livia, for example. Had she not attended the conference in town, Hiram and she may have never been reunited." He dished out another scoop of blood pudding. "Purely an act of fate. God's plan, if you will."

"Possibly," Naomi said and sighed, postponing any further interrogation. A part of her really did not want to know if Edward was involved in the Quinn scandal, the other demanded it.

After dinner, Hiram led Livia from the dining room to the hall. He stopped and removed his pocket watch. "It is time, Livy."

"Time for what?" *A proposal* she prayed.

"Your surprise."

"Oh." She tried to conceal her momentary disappointment.

"Close your eyes and hold my hand. I am leading you out to the porch."

New hope of the "surprise" heightened with each step down the hall. "This is so exciting," she whispered, as she heard the door open. Hiram led her outside.

"Open them, Livy."

Livia stood there, staring. A lump moved into her throat and tears instantly streamed down her cheeks. She could not speak; she could not move.

Hiram, too, was speechless, not quite sure of her response. The next second left no question to her feelings.

"This is the most regal, gorgeous specimen I have ever seen," she sniffled. "The color of his coat, the face, the perfect conformation," she mumbled.

"He is all yours, Livy."

"Oh, *Hiram.*" She walked over and reached up to run her fingers down the smooth, white face of the red sorrel Saddlebred. "His eyes are so gentle." She stroked his velvet muzzle.

"You have a lot in common."

"Do you think my eyes are gentle, too?" she grinned, not moving them from her beloved present.

"Yes, but I was referring to the fact that he, too, is an American. He just arrived."

"Hiram, what is his name?" she asked excitedly.

"Baron."

"Of course," she looked the horse over, "a noble title for the perfect gentleman." She moved in and put her arms around the horse's neck. "Welcome home, Baron," she whispered into his ear. "I shall always love you."

"And he you, Livy."

Behind the mansion, Guillaume asked Allison to stroll with him in the garden. He offered her his arm. "It was very generous of you to befriend Mercy, Allison."

"She is a very likeable person. I enjoy her company. Sophia and I are not as close as we used to be."

"Well, then, I guess her arrival came at an opportune time. I do wish you and Sophia got along better, but when I met Mercy I knew the two of you would get along famously."

"I hope this rift with Tavy does not deter her from staying."

"Yes, curious. I wonder about their history."

"Nothing pleasant, it would seem."

They turned to the path leading to the fountain.

"Allison, I have done a great deal of thinking on the road. A tremendous responsibility comes with this fortune. I would like you to be the first to know that I will not let it drastically convert my life."

"Indeed?"

"I do not plan to disrupt the McDonnally household, nor do I plan to live like a king or even like Hiram and Edward. I will pursue my career as an architect and enjoy life—the simple things. I hope that you understand."

She squinted with confusion. This statement she did not understand, but the next, she did.

He stopped and turned to face her. "Allison, only one thing is important to me. That is, that I share my new life with *you*." He reached into his pocket and pulled out a small velvet box.

"A dream you dream alone is only a dream.
A dream you dream together is reality."

Non-fictional facts referenced in Geoffrey's Secret

Timberclad home and hunting lodge construction
H.G. Wells' *The Invisible Man* (1897)
London Aerodrome factory and flying field for the
RAF (Royal Air Force) in Barnet/ London's NW side
Royal Ordinance Factory-arms and ammunition
(largest in Europe-30,000 women employees) in
Greenwich, London

Britain's *The Pall Mall Magazine, Housing Magazine*
Russian Matryoshka nesting dolls and origin, etc.
Dala Haus, Swedish wooden painted horse
Popularity of miniature stove, pots, and pans
Use of monacle and wired rim-spectacles
Duchess of Roxburghe (Miss Goelet) facts
Tolstoy's "Anna Karenina" (1873)
H.G. Wells' "The Time Machine" (1895)
G&W Grossmith's "Diary of a Nobody" (1892)
Caboc cheese from Scotland's western Highlands
Kilcaldy linoleum floor covering factory
Cox brothers'—largest Jute Factory in Lochee
Exeter in Devin, southern England
Essence of Cinnamon and Quinine—cold and flu
Germans take Brussels, Belgium Aug.20-23, 1914
Emperor of Japan declare war on Germany —
Aug.23, 1914
Robert Browning's *Lost Mistress* poem
Regent's Park—London Zoo
Location of Selby
Ailsa Shipbuilding & Engineering Co. Ltd., East
Ayrshire, Scotland— working with Royal Navy
DORA Act (Defense of the Realm Act) facts
"Baron", American Saddlebred

Poetry Excerpts from the Chapters

I   "Earl Richard"

II   "Yesterdays"

III Quote by St. John Chrysostom

IV   "A Better Resurrection"

V   "Suspense"

VI   "Discipline"

VII Quote of freed Latin slave (1B.C.)

VIII "The Fire of Drift-Wood"

IX   Adapted from Matthew 7:15

X   Proverbs 12:19

XI   "Mary's Lamb"

XII Read before a Teacher's Association at Pardeeville, WI 1871

XIII Proverb

XIV From "King Lear"

XV   Psalm 23:6

     Quote by John Lennon

Acknowledgements

British English A to Zed. New York: Facts on File, Inc., 2001.

Chronicle of the 20th Century. New York: Chronicle Publications, 1987.

Grun, Bernard. The Timetables of History: A Horizontal Linkage of People and Events. New York: Simon and Schuster, 1982.

Illustrated Encyclopedia of Scotland. Anacortes: Oyster Press, 2004.

Kidd, Dorothy. To See Ourselves. Edinburgh: HarperCollins, 1992.

Kirkby, Mandy. Pick Your Brains About Scotland. London: Cargan Guides, 2005.

Lacayo, Richard & Russell, George. Eyewitness 150 Years of Journalism. New York: Time Inc. Magazine Company, 1995.

Lochhead, Marion. Portrait of the Scott Country. London: The Trinity Press, 1968.

Summers, Gilbert. Exploring Rural Scotland. Lincolnwood: Passport Books, 1996.

This Fabulous Century Volume I and II. New York: Time-Life Books, 1969.

Webster's New Explorer Desk Encyclopedia. Springfield, MA: Federal Street Press, 2003.

Worthington-Williams, Michael. The Scottish Motor Industry. Great Britain: Shire Publications Ltd.,1989

Old News www.oldnewspublishing.com

I am a firm believer in that education
should be an ongoing endeavor.
I stand by the unwritten law that education
should be entertaining for young and old, alike.
Thus, I incorporate
historic places, people, and events in my novels,
for your learning pleasure.

With loving thoughts,
Arianna Snow

To order copies
of the
Lochmoor Glen Series

Visit the
Golden Horse Ltd.
website:
www.ariannaghnovels.com

Watch for the
eleventh in the series!